10/31/08

Pooh,

Have a happy Halloween. I love you very much. I hope you enjoy the book & it brings us a little extra cash. Maybe we can go somewhere cool.

This is the very first time I'm writing this in a book.

May you awaken from all your nightmares!

THE LOBBY

THE LOBBY

CHRISTOPHER A. DURISH

Sense of Wonder Press
JAMES A. ROCK & COMPANY, PUBLISHERS
ROCKVILLE • MARYLAND

The Lobby by Christopher A. Durish

SENSE OF WONDER PRESS
is an imprint of James A. Rock & Company, Publishers

The Lobby copyright ©2008 by Christopher A. Durish

Special contents of this edition copyright ©2008
by James A. Rock & Co., Publishers

Cover Illustration designed by Christopher A. Durish

All applicable copyrights and other rights reserved worldwide. No part of this publication may be reproduced, in any form or by any means, for any purpose, except as provided by the U.S. Copyright Law, without the express, written permission of the publisher.

This is a work of fiction. Names, characters, places and incidents either are the product of the author's imagination or are used fictitiously. Any resemblance to actual events, locales, organizations, or persons, living or dead, is entirely coincidental and beyond the intent of either the author or the publisher.

Note: Product names, logos, brands, and other trademarks occurring or referred to within this work are the property of their respective trademark holders.

Address comments and inquiries to:
SENSE OF WONDER PRESS
James A. Rock & Company, Publishers
9710 Traville Gateway Drive, #305
Rockville, MD 20850
E-mail:
jrock@rockpublishing.com   lrock@rockpublishing.com

Internet URL: www.rockpublishing.com

ISBN-13/EAN: 978-1-59663-615-6

Library of Congress Control Number: 2007936161

Printed in the United States of America

First Edition: 2008

Dedicated to

my wife

Melanie

and

my mother

Beverly

who is with me

in spirit

Acknowledgements

First, I would like to thank my wife, Melanie, who is the true inspiration behind everything I do. I would also like to thank God for giving me the gifts of creativity and storytelling that allowed me to start this book and the will power it required to finish it. Finally, I wish to thank all the fine people at James A. Rock Publishing who presented me with the opportunity to share this story with others who have the rather peculiar desire to be frightened.

This book is especially dedicated to the two women who have most influenced me as a writer and a person. To my beautiful wife, Melanie, who will always be my partner, in this life and beyond. And to my mother, who is with me now only in spirit, but who I know is still happier and more proud than anyone that I have finally realized the dream of being a published writer.

INTRODUCTION

*It is only the man absent of thought
who indeed can be absent of sin.
But only he who is absent of faith
cannot purge the demons within.*

There is a story in here somewhere, a tale of inevitable madness. An ordinary man, maybe someone just like you, slipping slowly from sanity's grip and into a realm far too horrible to imagine. A place of sinners, those who have squandered that which could have redeemed them. Salvation, abandoned or sold, for fortune or favor. Tokens of desire, collected in the pockets of he who has guided their eternal fate. A place where broken angels fly on the soiled wings of deception and greed and lust. Such a place beckons those who stray too far.

Misery is what you crave, and so you shall be fed. Digest what you wish or what is forced upon you. Maybe they are one and the same. The human mind can be perverse that way. A feast of flesh and blood, of pain and suffering. A last supper? Perhaps, for some, those too bloated to relieve themselves of all they have consumed.

Life is nothing more than death's finality undefined and each of us, merely a hostage. The only question is … from where will our ransom come?

Graffiti off the asylum wall.

WALLS CLOSING IN
CROWDING BLOOD SOAKED RECOLLECTION
NESTLED IN THIS TORMENT ANOTHER DAY
A TASTE OF SIN
THICK ON THE TONGUE OF CANNIBAL LUST
CHOKING BACK THE BREATH OF SANITY
SWALLOWING MINUSCULE TOKEN REMAINS OF SUCH
A LUNATIC'S PRAYERS
DISEASED WET SYLLABLES
COLLECTED ON THE CEILING OF A
GRAND CATHEDRAL
OH WHY DID I ABANDON THEE MY LORD
FOR NOW I AM SIMPLE PREY
CRIMSON SOLDIERS
THEY HAVE COME TO CLAIM MY SOILED SOUL
ETERNAL SLUMBER

ESCAPE

PEACE

MERCY

Saturday, 12:34 A.M.
Quinville State Medical Institution, New York

    A Roman Catholic Minister, committed two days prior, was found dead in his cell by a guard conducting midnight rounds. His naked body lay chest down on the floor, at the base of the room's padded rear wall. Surveillance video revealed disturbing footage of the priest charging the wall head first, like a mad bull, in a successful attempt to take his own life. The guard could still read the expression of morbid surrender on the victim's face and the final traces of insanity in the wide, vacant gaze cast back toward him.

A sinister suicide note was scrawled in blood on that wall, blood from fingers which the priest had chewed to the bone for no apparent reason other than he had been denied an ink pen and paper earlier that evening. The word "*MERCY*" was smudged at the point of impact, where his skull had struck the wall with enough force, and at just the right angle, to break the neck. A smeared trail of the fresh blood extended down to the white padded floor where the priest's twisted head had settled. He had been heard some hours earlier begging forgiveness for unspeakable acts and making claims that soldiers of Satan had been sent from Hell to collect his soul.

Chapter One

Four years later

Silence was broken by the voice of a man, and as he spoke, the secrets of his soul were revealed. *"Oh, night sky, royal ruler of dreams, lit by the moon queen. She has given birth to a billion shooting stars, diamond princes on invisible steeds."*

A finely chiseled sculpture of youth, the poet lay on his back, staring up at the brilliant scene sketched on the canvas of darkness hovering over them. He arose into a sitting position on the grass beside his lover as she collected the weight of his heavy vision from above.

She was beautiful, like Shakespeare's Juliet; and the beauty she possessed was not the bottled variety that clings to a wash cloth at the end of the day. No, she was truly one of God's masterpieces, a work of art whose grace transcended that of any worldly creation.

As she rested there against the earth, on a mattress of green, he began brushing strands of auburn hair from her face, uncovering the prominence of her cheekbones. He took a sip from the glass of Chardonnay next to a red rose on the ground beside him, then gently placed the rose by her ear. *"Swallow, take and make me hollow. I will follow. Relieve, receive me. All I give you, all you need, make me bleed, become your greed."*

The recital stopped. He began to undo the buttons of her dress. She was still. As he leaned over to learn the fullness of her lips, the fingers of his right hand explored more forbidden places, secrets not exposed by the dim light of the moon. She was cold. She was silent. She was, in fact … *dead*.

There was a silver dagger next to the shovel he had used to exhume the recently buried corpse of his lost love. He picked it up and pressed it to his broad chest with just enough force to puncture the skin. A single drop of blood trickled down to his bare navel. The cemetery around him grew restless in anticipation as he extended his muscular arms out in front of him, the tip of the dagger's shiny blade destined for his fractured heart. He cried out as he tightened his two-fisted grip around the pearl white crucifix that was its handle. *"Where night meets day, in that something less than splendid gray, I have lingered."*

Suddenly, just as he was about to bury the shiny blade deep into the cavity of his masculine chest, the eyes of his departed mate opened wide and she whispered a single word … *"Resurrection."*

* * *

The extensive eighty-two inch screen went black as the projection television, built directly into the wall, digested the final moments of Zachary Bell's creation. Judith Sample, a tall slender red head wearing a sophisticated navy business suit, flicked a switch on the rear wall and soft fluorescent light spilled out over the massive conference table, replacing the darkness that had briefly occupied each corner of the board room. She then strutted provocatively to the opposite side of the room, a lustful stare frozen on Zach the entire way. She seductively twirled open the Venetian blinds, allowing the vivid New York morning to settle in around her. "Absolutely brilliant," she mouthed silently, every syllable traced with meticulous indecency.

Zach certainly valued Judith's opinion … well, not really. But he did value the way the sunlight traced her flawless curves as she stood in front of the window. He wondered if his client felt the same, about his work that was. It was obvious by their kenneled-puppy stares that everyone at the table shared his appreciation of Judith's

THE LOBBY

flowing physique. Even the other two females in the room gazed at her as feelings of inferiority swelled, and not in the right places. Did they, however, agree with her evaluation of his commercial?

Seven people were seated around the table and yet, there was silence. Was this a good thing? Nervous anticipation boiled inside him. This was a giant account and he wanted desperately to nail it. Then someone spoke.

"Well, we didn't pay for the Pillsbury Doughboy," assured the deep authoritative voice of Raymond Reese, the sixty-seven year old president of Andromeda Enterprises, maker of Resurrection, a brand new fragrance for him and her.

Excitement on hold. Not quite there yet.

"I love it. It's got balls, exactly what we need to sell this shit!"

Excitement activated.

"Sir, but don't you think it's a bit …" the stuffy balding gentleman sitting next to Mr. Reese paused, "… a bit much?"

Confirmation necessary.

"Don't be silly, Wilson. It's exactly what we need." Reese emphasized the word *exactly* to Stanley Wilson, the attorney who had accompanied him to every business-related event in which he had been involved since he took over his father's fashion empire eleven years ago. "Our main target isn't those pups in the network audience. This stuff is pure Spike TV, the Playboy Channel."

Bingo!

Zach's confidence was justified, his brilliance reaffirmed. As a matter of fact, this might mean partner status at age thirty two, or at the very least, Rangers' season tickets. Andromeda was a huge account and securing it could propel the firm to the top of the advertising arena.

"Well, thank you, sir," Zach offered, his voice laced with relief.

INK Advertising, a six year old company dominated by hip, thirty something execs, had a reputation for producing commercials with a sharp edge. That is precisely why Zach left the stuffy bureaucracy that was the Brooke McCulley Agency eleven months ago. His work was bold, innovative, and sometimes hardcore; it always seemed to create tons of controversy over there that had them reaching for the sanctuary of their coffee mugs. His former colleagues had found it easier to swallow that last mouthful of cold decaf than to discuss his provocative creativity.

Artistic license, not financial gain, is what lured Zach to INK. Yes, he was pulling down thirty grand more than he had been with his previous employer, but it was a certain perk that INK offered, one that didn't come in his previous benefits package, that made them so attractive. An open mind.

They never rejected his work because it was too lewd. In fact, they considered it fresh and unequivocally brilliant. That is why they hired him the moment he came knocking. And so did their clients. That is why he was given the Andromeda account, the biggest in the company's relatively short history. They never whispered behind his back in disgust about what he considered art, disgust that, for half of those assholes at BM, was nothing more than disguised jealousy. Bottom line, he grabbed the attention of his clients, and their money; and now he was doing it for someone who didn't chastise him as they counted all the cash he brought in.

The boardroom emptied out into a large hallway stamped with a portfolio of ad campaign posters. Larry Tesh, a robust twenty nine-year-old exec who shared Zach's flair for the risqué, but with somewhat less success, approached him at the water cooler. "So?"

"What do you think?" Zach failed to suppress an egotistic grin.

"You got em, didn't you? Congratulations you son of a bitch, you did it again."

"And don't I always?"

Just then, Judith Sample swaggered past them flashing Zach that "let's do it right here on the floor while everyone's watching" glance. He winked in response as she turned the corner into her office. He placed a floral patterned Dixie cup under the blue nozzle of the Polar water tank and, as cool H2O filled the cup, he looked at Larry and smiled fiendishly.

Larry patted Zach on the right shoulder, "Always!" he muttered in a slightly jealous tone.

Raymond Reese approached as Larry wandered away, pondering just how fiery redheads really are in the sack. "Mr. Bell, or should I say Mr. Genius?" Reese laughed as he extended a hand toward Zach. "I was wondering if you had any plans for tomorrow evening." The man's handshake was firm but his hand was soft. Probably hadn't done an honest day's labor his whole life.

"Well, I don't believe …"

"Great!" Reese interrupted. "I am throwing a little shindig at my mansion in the hills tomorrow evening and you are cordially invited. In fact, I insist."

When a client of Raymond Reese's magnitude insisted, you simply did not refuse, no matter how graciously. "Sure, I wouldn't miss it," Zach accepted.

What the hell. This could be a prime opportunity for him to meet a lot of bigwigs, future clients, perhaps. Besides, Reese was rumored to throw one mean bash, not that Zach knew anyone personally who had ever been invited to one. He wasn't even quite sure where he had heard that rumor.

Raymond Reese was an imposing man who carried his age well. He was six foot four with distinguishing gray hair but looked closer to forty than seventy. He dressed like wealth, walked like wealth, even smelled like it. Billionaires do have those tendencies.

He summoned a piece of scrap paper from the pocket of his double breasted suit and proceeded to jot "1023 Haven Crest Lane" across it, ignoring the guidance of its blue lines. "Here's the address. Just take the Interstate north into Shamrock Grove, and then follow the signs to Shamrock Grove Country Club." He folded the paper and placed it in Zach's palm. "I'm a mile or so past the entrance on the left. 7 P.M. Oh, and bring that tasty little strawberry dish along with you," he added with a wink, referring to Judith Sample. And, even though Zach was a married man, his intention was to do exactly that.

The others had been mere flings, spontaneous one-nighters born of hormones and booze and survived only by clouded specs of memory and an incessant head pounding silenced by mid-afternoon.

Zach's affair with the twenty seven-year-old administrative assistant was different. Oh, it had begun as the previous ones had. *The lie* … a late night at the office working diligently to satisfy some fictional deadline. *The truth* … an early morning romp, working diligently to satisfy some sexual hunger before passing out in a strange bed.

The result with Ms. Sample, however, was not simply a phone number scrawled on a cocktail napkin and purposely misplaced as not to become evidence of any wrongdoing. It was, instead, a steamy affair conceived nine months earlier at Joe Guffy's retirement party and still very much alive on those occasional "late nights at the office." For Zach, Judith Sample's bed was anything but strange and tomorrow, it seemed, would definitely be one of those "late nights at the office."

Chapter Two

Tomorrow

A soft sunlight peeked shyly through her blinds, sprinkling her room with only the slightest hint of dawn and yet; little Aria Bell popped up from her pillow with an innocent exuberance to rival that of any normal eight-year-old … on Christmas morning.

She stepped into her Cookie Monster slippers, both feet at once and, even though it was a school day and Santa wasn't due for more than three months, she raced down the spiral staircase as if a plethora of presents awaited her. Normally, it was her six-year-old sister who greeted school day mornings with such enthusiasm. Dove was only a first grader and had not yet experienced the day to day hustle and bustle of the third grade.

Today, however, was no ordinary day. Aria had been anticipating this day for nearly a month; for it was on this fine day that she was to become a star. She had crossed out the previous twenty six squares on her Little Mermaid calendar, which was tacked to the wall above her Little Mermaid desk, and finally reached the one that read *"THE LION KING"* in purple crayon.

Albert Einstein Elementary School was presenting its rendition of the beloved Disney tale at eight o'clock in the school auditorium and Aria had secured a prominent part as Nala, the feline princess. A month of hard work that began even before the new school year started was finally going to pay off.

She followed the scent of a good old-fashioned country breakfast that led her toward the kitchen. On her way through the living room, she snatched an orange booklet that read *"THE LION KING* Script" from the mantle above the white brick fireplace.

"Morning mommy," she offered vigorously as she traipsed into the kitchen.

"Good morning sweetie. Aren't we chipper this morning?"

As she propped herself up onto a chair at the kitchen table, Aria rehearsed the last few lines of Act II, letting out a majestic "roar" as she scooped a serving of scrambled eggs from a large wooden bowl onto her plate.

"Watch sweetie, don't burn yourself," Katie Bell warned before turning her attention to the other family members who had not yet made their way downstairs. "Breakfast is ready you sleepy heads!" she announced with a shout as she pulled a tray of steaming biscuits from the oven. The tray's heat penetrated the canary yellow potholder in her left hand and she quickly placed it on the counter. "Ouch!" she muttered, trying to shake the burn from her fingers.

"Hot mommy?" Aria questioned, reaching for one of the biscuits.

"Yes honey, don't touch until they've cooled a bit."

The Bell family resided in a stately five bedroom Colonial located in a sparsely populated town separated from the Big Apple by forty-two mostly uneventful miles. It was sided in Document Gray vinyl; the color one might see threading the suit of an aging congressman. It had, however, been brought to life by an assortment of trees and a delicately patterned floral arrangement created by Katie herself and still clinging to rich colors that the chill of Fall would soon strip away. The old house, which Katie and Zach had purchased from an elderly couple who was looking to down size, had been occupied for all but one of its fifty years, and five decades of yapping had corroded whatever sound barrier the hardwood floors and ten foot ceilings may have provided in their younger days.

Dove prodded down the steps and across the family room as if all 101 Dalmatians were cuddled up inside her tiny black and white polka-dotted slippers. She stumbled into the kitchen as she attempted to rub a fresh dream from her eyes and joined the other two women of the house who had already settled into the day's routine.

"Good morning miss," Katie greeted her youngest daughter.

Dove managed a halfhearted "morning" and then continued to rub her eyes as she took her place next to Aria at the table.

Unlike her sister, whose physical appearance mocked the lofty stature, deep brown eyes, and curly walnut hair of her father, Dove was a petite echo of her thirty-year-old mother. She possessed Katie's contemporary beauty … her Caribbean blue eyes, slender form, and angular but not overly protruding chin. She even wore her hair, a slightly gentler shade of blonde than her mother's, in the same charismatic shoulder length style that barely harbored the secrets of Katie's sensual nape.

Mojo, the family dog who usually spent his mornings trying to bribe a few scraps from the breakfast table, seemed a bit preoccupied with something in the back yard. He stood staring out through the screen door, his lean, well-developed frame stock still as he whimpered softly. The six-year-old Jack Russell was named after Zach's favorite musician, Jim Morrison, who inspired the dark edge in his commercials. "His alphabet would never float in soup," Zach would say of The Doors' flamboyant front man. "But rather, it would sink to the bottom of the bowl until all the broth was consumed."

Katie opened the screen door, allowing Mojo access to the fenced in acre behind the house, then turned her attention back inside as the dog darted from a complete standstill into a frenzied dash across the lawn. "C'mon Zach!" she shouted at the ceiling. "Your eggs are gonna sprout feathers and fly up there to you."

This comment provoked further scrutiny from the always inquisitive Dove. "Mommy, can chickens really fly? I never saw one up in the air before."

"No honey, chickens …"

"Of course not silly, and neither can pigs," Aria interrupted, chomping on a slice of bacon.

"Then why do they have wings smarty pants, huh?" Dove's challenge was laced with a sarcasm that topped even her sister's. "Maybe they fly while we're sleeping."

"The wings are just for decoration, stupid."

"Hey, knock it off you two," Katie intervened, waving a wooden spoon in the air like a fly swatter, or maybe, a flying pig swatter. "Finish breakfast before you're late for the bus."

Fifteen minutes elapsed before Zach, his modestly masculine physique packaged in his most expensive three-piece suit, hustled into the kitchen. The gel in his towel dried curls had only begun to stiffen the style in place as he bee-lined for the coffee pot and coaxed every last drop of Java into the sealable Sunoco mug he plucked from the cabinet above.

"Aren't you going to eat something?" Katie questioned in a tone that suggested she already knew the answer.

"I'm in a bit of a rush dear," he paused, scampering toward the table. "But I will have one of these biscuits."

"At least put some eggs in that thing," she offered. Zach hurtled that suggestion as if it were simply a ploy to slow him down.

"Daddy, tell Dove chickens can't fly," Aria said, refueling the poultry debate.

"No pumpkin, chickens can't fly." He sliced the biscuit in half with a butter knife and crammed the entire lid of the hot pastry into his mouth. The unexpected burn did not allow him to begin chewing for several painful seconds.

Aria copped one of those "I told you so" grins and Dove quickly flashed her tongue in retort.

"I gotta go or I'll be late … all that damned road construction." Zach stuffed the other half of the biscuit in his mouth, then plucked the coffee mug and a black briefcase from the counter. He scurried toward the door that connected the kitchen with the garage.

"Yeah, I guess it is that time of the year," Katie responded as she undid her green and white striped apron and draped it over the back of her chair.

"Bye girls, love you," Zach managed through the remainder of his biscuit.

Katie trailed him and a duet of sugar coated "love you too" down the steps and into the garage. "Don't forget your daughter's acting debut tonight," she reminded as Zach climbed into his dark green Lexus which was parked next to her silver Honda Accord and amongst a variety of tools and gadgets hung neatly on peg hooks that lined the walls of the garage. Some of the tools had never been used. Some, he didn't even know how to use. He wasn't exactly what one would call a handyman. He was, however, one of those guys who had to have every new gizmo that popped up on some infomercial at two in the morning.

"Oh shit, that's right … damn it!" Zach lowered his head and closed his eyes, "I have to meet a very important client for a late dinner, just business." What he really should have been saying was, "I'll be out till 3 A.M. screwing another woman."

Katie raised her eyebrows toward her hairline and when they dropped a few seconds later, Zach knew exactly what was coming. Faces are easy to read after nine years of marriage.

"Don't even start Kate," he warned with one foot in the car and one out.

"Damn it, Zach, you know how important this is to her. How can you be so damn self centered?"

"Self centered? Who in the hell do you think I'm …" Zach's rebuttal stalled as the car's engine fired up. "I don't have time to argue with you Kate." It was always *Kate*, not Katie, during arguments; and they had definitely been having their share of those lately. "You're going to videotape it, right? So just tell her I promise to watch it with her tomorrow night, okay?"

"Yeah, you promise! Why do I always have to be the bearer of your fucking bad tidings?" Katie snapped, swearing uncharacteristically as she ground her teeth into an intolerant scowl. She was normally quite the pacifist. But when Zach put his work above her and the girls, especially the girls—and he seemed to be doing a lot of that lately as well—it definitely rubbed her the wrong way.

Zach pulled his other leg inside the car and slammed the door shut a little harder than normal. "Just tell her, okay? I gotta go. I'll watch it tomorrow." The glass from the window and the grind from the automatic garage door opening behind him muffled his words.

Zach backed onto Grouse Run and proceeded left down Crabtree Lane, the gravel extension that formed the T at the curb in front of the house. Katie stood at the peak of the driveway with her arms pulled into her chest and her astute figure framed by the open garage. As he sped off, he could see her waning reflection in the rearview mirror and could feel the emphasis of her indignant glare on his shoulder. He only shrugged it off as he drove out of her sight toward the city.

Chapter Three

The Reese mansion sat back off the road some two hundred yards, far removed from the occasional grumble of RVs heading north toward a mountain retreat in the Catskills. A secret harbored for more than a century by a fortress of unkempt brush and pine, the substantial stone structure was rarely seen by the uninvited.

Norway Pines straddled the gravel extension that stretched to the property, and as Zach drove slowly between them, he was filled with both awe and uncertainty. He admired the ghostly serenity provided by the dense green wall of foliage all the while contemplating whether he had turned off at the right place.

Judith was oblivious to the natural beauty that surrounded her and was, instead, completely absorbed in the cosmetic beauty reflected in the mirror of her compact.

"This is amazing, so peaceful," Zach observed aloud.

Judith lifted her head up momentarily then glanced, unimpressed, out the window of the Lexus. "Are you sure this is it?" she questioned as she dropped her eyes back down and continued to touch up her makeup. "I was expecting Bill Gates, not Daniel Boone."

"This must be it," Zach answered when a towering black wrought iron gate came into view thirty feet ahead.

He pulled up to the black box that stood a few feet from the gate and stopped. He pressed a small white button and a few seconds later the box spoke. "Last name sir?" a voice crackled in a polished British accent.

"Bell ... Zachary Bell."

Several moments of awkward silence expired before the voice returned. "Oh yes, very well. Please pull forward when the gate opens."

The grand gate slowly swung open and Zach drove through, peering up at the pointed tips of the slender iron bars that shot toward the sky like arrows aimed at the heavens. He watched in the rearview mirror as the gate closed and couldn't help but feel as if he and Judith had just entered Oz.

The corner of the mansion peeked out from behind the tree line and, as they continued along the yellow brick road—it was actually a black tar road—the entire awe-inspiring image began to unfold before them. Now Judith was impressed. "Wow, look at this place!" she gushed, gazing at the palatial residence as her disc of facial dust nearly slipped from her fingers. "I've only seen houses like this in the movies."

"Houses?" Zach let out a sarcastic grunt. "This is a freaking castle. We're talking full scale fairy tale here."

"You weren't kidding when you said this guy was loaded." Judith flipped the lid shut on her compact and tucked it away in her purse.

"Yeah, I guess not, huh?"

A majestic landscape of Kentucky bluegrass had been carved into the wilderness amongst the humble lodgings of four-legged neighbors. Sharp rows of Aster traced concrete trails. Tiger Lilies prowled patches of red cedar mulch and a cluster of wild Honeysuckle gathered by a tranquil stream to bathe in the last rays of evening sun. It was a collaboration of man and Mother Nature and the border formed at the wood line was both seamless and abrupt.

The mansion itself, a classic Georgian Colonial, was a truly mythical structure consisting of a magnificent central edifice flanked by two smaller twin buildings, probably used as guest or servant quarters. This stately triumvirate was the centerpiece of the grandiose estate, and as the approaching car rolled slowly toward it; the imposing ivy covered facade of stone and brick filled the windshield.

Attic dormers, capped with alternating arched and triangular pediments, protruded out from the shingled roof, and two brick chimneys stood guard behind them.

Judith and Zach felt overwhelmed and a bit giddy, like children taking that first ferry ride to Disney World. Just ahead, the Magic Kingdom awaited. The expansive driveway ushered them to a massive slab of asphalt that rivaled the parking lot at the shopping mall but was embellished with mostly imports, Jags, Mercedes, Beemers, and even a vintage 1969 Rolls Royce Silver Shadow. A large cul-de-sac at the end of the driveway showcased a mammoth fountain from which frothing red and purple water spurted to Tchaikovsky's *1812 Overture*.

"Look at that awesome fountain," Judith remarked as a teenage boy in a black tuxedo stepped into view with his left hand extended out in front of him.

"I wouldn't be surprised if that was Champagne shooting outta there." Zach stopped the car next to the valet attendant. He straightened the bow tie on his own tux as the dapper young man in the driveway opened the passenger door for Judith.

"Good evening ma'am."

"Thank you very much." Judith stepped out of the car, allowing the hem of her full length black sequin dress to fall elegantly around her ankles.

Zach got out before the valet attendant could shuffle around to extend the same courtesy to him. He held out a ten-dollar bill but the young man refused politely. "That is not necessary sir," the boy explained in a tone uncharacteristically proper for a teenager. "I am paid extremely well."

"I'll bet you are," Zach said as he stuffed the bill back into his wallet.

"Besides, I get to drive all of these really cool cars, even if it is just around the driveway." Now, that sounded more like a teenage boy.

Zach smiled and took Judith by the hand as they ascended a set of concrete steps, seven in all and flanked by pillars of vine covered cement. He turned to note the exact location of his parked Lexus, even though he would not have to retrieve it after the party; then he pressed the illuminated doorbell and stood back to admire the intricate detail carved into the Tuscan doorway and the curves of the Palladian window that capped it. A few seconds later, the door swung inward and a tuxedo-clad gentleman in his sixties greeted them. "Good evening ma'am, sir, do come in." This was the same English voice that gave life to the rusting box at the black iron gate.

"Thank you." Judith and Zach stepped into a grand foyer as the butler closed the door behind them. They lingered for a moment, gazing in awe at the vast array of artwork that dignified the significant walls surrounding them. The room had the flatulent, hollow feel of a museum. It gave both of them chills.

"Wow!" Zach whispered as he nudged Judith's arm softly. "I think that's a van Gogh," he motioned with his head toward an early work of the nineteenth century Impressionist. It portrayed a fruit bat with its wings fully extended and the light of a candle framing their intricate color scheme from behind.

"*Flying Fox.*" the butler confirmed. "And that one over there is '*Self Portrait With A Felt Hat*', all Master Edition Proofs ... Now if you'll follow me, the others have already begun to mingle in the main parlor." The butler proceeded like a British soldier toward the party as Zach peeled his eyes from the paintings and followed Judith who was trailing closely behind their temporary tour guide.

Amazing! Zach admired inwardly. He knew little about European art but was fairly certain that anything done by someone he recognized had to be worth some serious coin.

The laughter and prattle of a festive gathering became more discernible as they walked through a room decorated with various knick-knacks that made Judith's collection of Swarovski crystal seem like clearance rubble from a Five and Dime. There were colorful oriental vases set inches apart in a shell-topped cupboard and solid gold chess pieces atop a game board spread out across a Queen Anne table. The strategic location of each piece suggested a game in progress.

Finally, after what seemed like several lengthy minutes of walking and gawking, the trio came to the arched entrance of the parlor. The butler stopped and raised his arm as the cuff of his white shirtsleeve pulled away to reveal a gold Rolex. "Here we are," he gestured with his hand.

"Nice watch!" Zach commented as the shiny timepiece reflected the light of the giant crystal chandelier that hung above the guests.

"Oh yes, it was an anniversary gift from Mr. Reese, ten years in his service last April."

"Some gift," Zach smiled.

He and Judith stepped just inside the vast room and immediately collected a barrage of judgmental glances from the snobby, high society types that seemed to be constantly assessing and secretly maintaining their personal space. There had to be about thirty of them, assembled in small cliques that crowded but did not congest the massive space above the cherry hardwood floor. They pecked like parakeets on ors-derves and sipped Dom Perignon as they stood by the unlit marble fireplace or around the coordinating white Baby Grand. It looked like a scene right out of the movie, *Titanic*.

"Zachary Bell," a familiar voice drew Zach's attention across the room and soon Raymond Reese emerged from the crowd wearing a gray double-breasted tuxedo and staggering slightly, as if his legs had already been filled to the kneecaps with bourbon. "Zachary, you made it, splendid!" Reese transferred the glass he was holding to his left hand, then grasped Zach's hand in a firm shake with the right. "Did you have any trouble finding the place?"

"Oh no, not at all, your directions were right on the mark," Zach assured, then paused for a moment to digest the grandeur of the event before continuing, "This is Judith Sample, Judith, Raymond Reese."

"It's a pleasure," Judith smiled politely and nodded.

The old man pulled her hand to his face and pressed his lips softly against her smooth knuckles, "A pleasure indeed, my dear. You are an absolutely ravishing spectacle this evening. I'm so pleased you could accompany Zachary to our little shindig."

There was something about the way Reese spoke, something different from the way Zach remembered. He had only conversed with him on two prior occasions; yesterday at the office and a month earlier during initial discussions about the Resurrection project, yet the change was quite obvious. He was rough and arrogant at those meetings, swearing like a Texas businessman who just struck oatmeal in an oil field. It was that crude gusto that had stood out above all else, that had defined this old man of utmost importance but little couth.

Now, however, Reese sounded much more sophisticated, proper, like the English butler who answered his door. Zach was surprised by this change, and a bit disappointed. In an odd way, he had found the billionaire's raw demeanor somewhat inspiring—a wealthy egotist who could say and do whatever he pleased. Just gawking around at the old man's house, however, offered a whole new inspiration.

"Come, let me introduce you to the others," Reese said as he placed his hand on Judith's shoulder, urging her a few steps forward. He took a gulp from the glass he held in the other hand, then raised the glass and his voice, "Pardon me, may I have everyone's attention for just a moment?" his words dissected loose chatter of stock market trends and country club politics. All at once, there was silence, except for the throaty cough of an older gentleman who leaned against the piano. "I would like to introduce Mr. Zachary Bell and his friend Miss Judith Sample." He turned to Judith and whispered, "It is *Miss* Sample, is it not?"

"Oh God, yes," she laughed.

Judith blushed and Zach nodded "hello" as they recaptured the examining eyes and insincere smiles of the group. It seemed the word "friend" in their host's introduction kindled a fair amount of curious speculation.

"This young fellow's brilliant ad campaign for my Resurrection fragrance is going to make a wealthy man even wealthier," Reese declared as he draped his arm around the back of Zach's neck and tugged him affectionately.

Unenthusiastic smiles and nodded gestures followed, insuring Zach and Judith's acceptance into the club, at least for the evening.

Chapter Four

The infant moon, which had been so radiant in the sky above Raymond Reese's mansion earlier that evening, was now several hours older and tucked away in a cradle of black clouds too tired to hold the weighty rain of a typically heavy September storm.

Zach was also having a difficult time keeping his eyes employable as the pounding lullaby of one too many Vodka Tonics clamored about his head. Still, he proceeded through the iron gate and down the private road that connected the Reese estate to the increasingly slick black top that stretched back to the city.

Judith, who had to be carried to the car because an obscenely expensive Jamaican rum called Brugal Siglo de Oro claimed her ability to walk erect several hours prior, was out cold in the passenger seat. Her contorted mass was slumped in such a position, back wedged into the cleft of the seat, neck chinked awkwardly against the window frame, she would certainly require a healthy dose of Ben Gay with her aspirin breakfast in the morning.

"I can make it," Zach convinced himself as he rubbed his eyes. No matter how tired or intoxicated, or both, he had been while driving in the past; he had always managed to reach his destination safely. He had convinced himself long ago that he was a better driver when he was drunk because he concentrated more to make up for sluggish reflexes and diminished motor skills. But even the words of his thoughts were slurred on this stormy night as he headed south through a thick wall of precipitation. The rain, which pilfered all sight beyond a few feet, and the absence of any salvation the high beams might provide, made it that much more difficult to decipher what vague instructions the yellow line in the center of the road offered. And so the emerald Lexus turtled along at a spitefully reluctant pace, as if a sudden dose of 5 P.M. city traffic just happened upon this rural stretch some seventy miles removed from anything resembling a well-traveled road.

Zach turned the air conditioner on full blast, adjusting the vents so that the refreshing chill blew directly at his face. That, and the company of four guys named Crosby, Stills, Nash, and Young, he figured, would keep him alert long enough to get back to Judith's downtown apartment. He would just crash there and worry about conjuring up some manufactured alibi to feed Katie in the morning. It certainly wouldn't be the first time.

"Helplessly hoping, her harlequin hovers nearby," Zach sang along as Judith slept. He glanced over at her and placed his right hand on her shoulder. She rustled briefly then was still again. He turned his weary eyes back to the road in front of him. It was hypnotic and pulled the lids down over his vision. He jerked his drooping head back up, regaining the road in his dilated pupils, and then slapped himself briskly across one cheek thinking that it would somehow energize him. He was wrong. The fourth track on the CD spilled into the fifth as Zach drifted off to sleep. It was at that moment that his nightmare began.

The image of a demon's face, possibly that of Satan himself, appeared to him in a few seconds worth of dreaming. Its skin was pale white, almost ghostlike, and ravaged by tiny cracks that jutted in all directions. Its mouth was foaming with bubbly yellowish saliva that coated its forked tongue and needle thin teeth. And its eyes were solid black and eerily seductive. Its eyes drew him in by the fear they induced.

"I am waiting for you my son," it whispered, "waiting to devour your soul."

"Noooooo," Zach bellowed as the car swerved from the road.

Suddenly, he awakened and, in the brief seconds of confused panic that followed, tramped on the break pedal with every ounce of force his right leg could muster. The thin sheet of water that had accumulated beneath them loosened the grip of the tires and the car began to hydroplane, spinning uncontrollably toward the road's edge. Every muscle in his body tightened like a stretched rubber band as the car slid over an unguarded embankment and began its decent. His ears absorbed only the first seconds of horrible "crunching" as brush surrendered to metal, then metal to earth, flipping and bouncing, before finally coming to rest in the wet grass some thirty five feet below. Then, all at once, an uneasy silence settled around the wreckage.

Judith never felt a thing. Not the shifting of her bones. Not the snapping of her neck. Her twisted Raggedy Ann remains were deposited in the back seat of the crumpled Lexus and, even though she had been violently tossed like linens in a clothes dryer, she never was, nor ever would be, shaken from the Rum-soaked slumber that was her anesthesia.

Zach, however, sat upright, pinned to the leather of the driver's seat by the steering wheel that pressed its signature into his chest. He was alive but, he too, was ignorant to pain. He suffered only for a brief moment when his skull struck the roof of the car, suffering which was instantly numbed by the resulting onslaught of unconsciousness.

Blood streamed from his nose and forehead and from the various lacerations carved into his face by the shards of windshield glass now strewn about in random imperfection across the lawn of an old farmhouse. It stained the crumpled air bag that served as a bib beneath his chin and the tattered clothing that clung to his bruised body.

The sounds of hissing smoke and settling steel interrupted the brief silence, then were joined by a distant quartet of barking hounds and the unmistakable squealing of a screen door begging for WD-40.

Eighty year old Gus Hadley, who had been stripped of his dreams by all the commotion, went out to investigate. His attire, a pair of thick cotton boxer shorts and black knee high socks, suggested that he had been in bed. The bottle of Scotch in his left hand confirmed that he wouldn't be returning anytime soon. He angrily swatted at the moths convening in the yellow glow of the porch light, as if he were certain that they were the ones directly responsible for the holes in his flannel robe. "Damn bugs," he mumbled as he crept across the soaked lawn in his stocking feet, clearing his throat as he approached the wreckage that had suddenly been cast from the darkness above.

"Is anyone in there? Hello, someone still alive in there?" He pulled the bottle to his face. The smooth rounded opening at the top fit his puckered lips like a puzzle piece. The rain had stalled to a steady sprinkle and began to plaster his few remaining white hairs to his head.

"Gut meet Scotch," he grunted as he gulped down a giant swig and belched. No introduction was necessary, however. The two had kept company many times before and were like family. The deep, rumbling, from-the-gut burp suggested a somewhat shaky in-laws type relationship, but family none the less.

"Hello ... hey can you hear me in there?" Gus walked a few steps closer, allowing a foggy view of Zach's mangled body to penetrate his cataracts and the rain splotched eyeglasses he rubbed against the sleeve of his robe. The sweet smell of antifreeze and the sharp scent of gasoline mingled in the air and stung his nostrils. He was a foot or two from the vehicle when he realized he would get no response from those inside.

He stared at the steel chamber a few moments more before he returned to the house to call the State Troopers. His wet socks dampened the linoleum of the kitchen floor as he trudged his way to the phone on the opposite wall. He dialed the number for the State Police as he pulled the phone cord back across the kitchen to the window above the sink, the one that opened to the backyard where the Lexus rested.

"State Police, Officer Lentz, can I help you?"

"Yeah, this is Gus Hadley. There's a damn foreign car on my front porch!" the old farmer explained, exaggerating distance by a good thirty yards. He guzzled down another mouthful of Scotch as though it were Kool Aid, wearing the face of a cowboy as the booze tugged at his taste buds but failed to coax even the slightest grimace. "Musta rolled down over the hill there, scared the milk right outta my heifers."

"Are you telling me there was an accident sir?" the young officer probed.

"That's what I'm a sayin son, glass and metal all over the damn place."

"And what about injuries? Is there anyone still inside the vehicle?"

"Yep, two folks I think, and they ain't lookin none too perdy either."

"Alright sir, we'll get someone out there right away."

The officer didn't need the address. The State boys were all too familiar with Gus Hadley. For a while there, after his wife had passed away of cancer, the old farmer took up moonshining in his basement. The boys caught wind of it and paid a little visit. They confiscated the stills and other equipment he used to produce his special recipe but didn't have it in them to arrest old Gus. They even let him keep a few jugs of the homemade juice he had stored away, what with his wife dying and all.

"The booze was better company," he had said once. "Put me to sleep almost as quick as her yappin."

Gus loved his wife dearly, however, and never really meant what he had said. Not entirely anyway.

The rain and approximately twenty-five minutes expired before an orchestra of sirens gave music to the ballet of smoke dancing from the grill of the Lexus. Shortly after that, the stage of brisk autumn air was decorated in flashes of blue and red.

* * *

Gus Hadley's property had become what would have been a spectacle had there been more observers looking on. A Life Flight helicopter settled onto a clear patch of the Hadley farm a short distance from the crumpled Lexus. People in uniform were everywhere, each one performing specific duties in a sloppily choreographed but deliberately efficient rescue. A short, stout female paramedic pulled an orange blanket over Judith Sample's face, then pushed her lifeless body into the back of an ambulance. The cover offered only superficial relief from the unforgettable image of dried blood that clung to her hair and the way her head just dangled from her shoulders like that of a scarecrow stuffed with too little straw ... *Guaranteed nightmares*.

A small group of passers-by had pulled their cars off to the side of the road and were now assembled at the edge of the old farmer's driveway. Four members of Fire Rescue utilized a devise that resembled a giant pair of tin snips to parole Zach from the metal prison that was once his 06 Lexus IS250.

Unlike Judith, who was easily extracted from the wreckage through the shattered rear window, Zach was trapped. He was unconscious and had lost a lot of blood, but life still stuck to him ... with scotch tape and paper clips.

"Pull that piece of the door frame away from him," said a graying man in his mid-fifties, the captain and elder member of the rescue team.

"Careful Chuck, real slow," instructed the twenty-nine year old who stood on the car's rippled hood to get a view the others didn't have.

"I know, I know." And with a deep breath and a firm but calculated tug, the piece was pried away.

"Now this piece that I just cut," the captain directed calmly.

A young strapping buck called Pipes, the rookie of the group with only one such rescue on his resume', peeled a second slab of the driver's door from the rest of the vehicle. Zach's mangled body shifted ever so slightly, causing the rescue team's already frayed nerves to split once more. Each member of the unit, however, remained composed and collected. They simply had to. A life most certainly depended on it.

"Easy does it, gently ... gently"

Finally, after forty minutes of tedious work, the rescue team pulled Zach from the wreckage, easing him face up onto the grass as the small throng of observers applauded. They slid a backboard underneath his limp body before stabilizing his head to prevent further injury.

"Okay, now let's get this man to the hospital."

Medics took over as the members of Fire Rescue were finally able to relax. The youngest, the one they called Pipes, dropped to the wet lawn with a sigh that suggested both relief and exhaustion.

The whipping sound of the helicopter's propeller once again cascaded the night sky with shrieking urgency as Zach was lifted off into the blackness, leaving below a circus of formalities that would continue well into the morning.

The audience, who had been held captive by the drama that had unfolded before them, drama they usually witnessed only on one of those "World's Scariest" programs, started to peel slowly away from the scene. On this night, they would drive a lot slower than normal and take with them disturbing memories they would not soon forget.

The helicopter rapidly dispatched thirty-two miles behind it and arrived at St. Margaret's Hospital in just under fifteen minutes. The medics had radioed ahead and a medical team including Dr. Martin Kim, one of the area's finest trauma surgeons, was prepared for and awaiting Zach's arrival.

Chapter Five

It was 1:23 A.M. when Zach arrived at Saint Margaret's and the belly of the massive building, which had been uncharacteristically settled for most of the night, rumbled as if it were rejecting rotten pork. The electronic doors swung open as the invisible butler seemed to sense the exigency of the approaching medics, one, a black male in his late twenties and the other, a white male whose acne gave him the appearance of a teenager. The overnight trauma team greeted the medics like second leg sprinters in a relay race and wheeled Zach swiftly down the Northeast corridor toward ER.

Dr. Kim, an American born man of Korean decent, appeared in green scrubs at the end of the hall. As the portable bed on which Zach laid and the hovering nurses that surrounded it moved closer, the doctor stepped back into the room from which he had emerged. After a few seconds, the patient and his medical entourage joined him in the operating room. The race to save Zach's life had just entered the critical turn.

✳ ✳ ✳

9:14 A.M.

Nearly eight hours later, the marathon was over. The surgery had gone as well as could be expected and Zach was out of immediate danger. Dr. Kim was able to halt the brain hemorrhaging that had threatened his life. He was, however, still in a coma from which he might never awaken. And even if he did, permanent brain damage was a very real possibility. Dr. Kim also repaired two broken ribs, a fractured left wrist, and the various lacerations that had been carved into his flesh by twisted metal and shattered glass.

Katie, who had been notified shortly after Zach arrived at Saint Margaret's, took the girls to her mother's on Long Island before driving to the hospital where her husband clung to life. She had arrived around 3 A.M. For the past six hours, significant thoughts, nearly unbearable at times, bounced back and forth in her brain like a ping pong ball.

Who was this woman who died in the crash? And what in the hell was she doing with Zach? Was he being unfaithful? If so, for how long? Would he live to tell her? Would he tell her the truth? Did she want to know the truth? *Would he live?* What if their last moments together were those in the garage as Zach left for work yesterday morning? What if their last conversation ended with the anger-laden obscenities she had hurled at him until the garage door opened and he sped off? Even though he had absolutely deserved it, she couldn't stand the thought of those being the last words she would ever say to him.

For the first hour, she had kept the company of an elderly couple in their sixties in the expansive waiting area. Their forty year old son had been in a motorcycle accident, serious, but as it turned out, not life threatening. They figured he was inebriated, probably on his way home from the bar. The idle chatter kept Katie's mind at least partially shielded from the angst that completely absorbed her after they left around four o'clock.

For the five enduring hours that ensued, it was only her, playing solitaire with her thoughts, and the aimless glares of the famous people whose faces decorated the tablecloth of outdated magazines beside her. She found little sanctuary in the tranquil scenes portrayed in the cheap Kmart paintings that accented the surrounding walls. Her eyes, which had been filtering the salty malaise of her tears throughout the morning, felt puffy and spent.

She adjusted the weight of her tight muscles, withdrawing an image from her memory bank as she settled into an equally uncomfortable position. This thought, however, was a good thought, her first in several hours.

A sun-washed grove of oak trees and the playful squirrels that chased from one to the next. It was a place she remembered well and she didn't have to stretch her mind for details. *A weathered wooden bench, the cheery tune of a robin welcoming summer, or the way the cool May breeze gently caressed her face as she and Zach pondered the great wide open that was their future together.* She could easily recall their very first day there, sitting on the lawn in front of the library as Zach timidly recited one of his poems. It was almost as if he were auditioning for her company.

"Where the sea meets the sky, blue on blue like the glance of an eye on some restless tide, washing to shore lost dreams that have died in the fathoms of time."

They had only been out on a few pizza-and-a-movie dates, but it didn't matter. On that day, he captured her heart ... forever.

"The sands, absorbing the tears that over the years have made deep and then deeper this ocean of pain."

She could detect a subtle shyness in his voice as he humbly revealed himself to her. Later that evening, she revealed herself to him for the first time.

He was a junior majoring in Jim Morrison and the non-medicinal benefits of pot. She, a sophomore majoring in the seasons and all of the gifts that youth offered. They met by chance really, at a University of Vermont baseball game. Neither was much of a baseball fan. Katie was there because a roomie, whose fiancé was the starting pitcher that game, had an extra ticket and pleaded with her for two days to go. Zach was the assistant editor of the school newspaper, covering for the regular sports reporter who came down with a nasty case of food poisoning.

The following spring, Zach graduated from UV and took a job with a small advertising agency in New York. Katie finished school that summer, cramming her final ten credits into two months worth of classes so that she could join Zach in the big city. Eight month's later, beneath the pattering of a light April shower; they exchanged the sacred vows of unity.

"Sacred," she muttered, her eyes once again swelling with tears as she was slammed back into the reality that was a lumpy naugahyde chair in the waiting room of St. Margaret's Hospital. Those famous faces were still gawking up at her from their paper prisons on the small wooden table beside her. She picked up the outdated issue of People and began to leaf aimlessly through the pages, trying unsuccessfully to ignore the negative thoughts that inevitably crept back into her head.

What if Zach didn't make it, how would she break it to the girls? She had told Dove and Aria that Daddy hurt himself but that he was going to be okay. What else could she have told them? But now, if he wasn't okay, how would she explain?

For the next several minutes, she thought only about Dove and Aria. That was, until *the* woman popped back into her head. What if she could never talk with Zach again, never find out the truth about where he was and the woman he was with? Even worse, if she did learn the truth and ... "Mrs. Bell?" a soft voice interrupted.

Katie peered up at Dr. Kim, instantly trying to anticipate his next words by translating the expression on his face. He greeted her with a forced smile and a concerned gaze; it was probably not good news.

"Hello, I'm Dr. Martin Kim. You are Zach's wife, correct?"

"Yes, yes I am." Katie sprung up from the chair as the room around her became a blur and her eyes latched on to the doctor's mouth. "How's my husband?"

"He's alive."

"Oh, thank ..."

Dr. Kim quickly intervened. "However, Mrs. Bell," he paused, "maybe you better sit down."

She dropped back down into her seat while Dr. Kim took the chair next to her.

"What is it Doctor? He's not going to make it, is he?" Katie started to sob again, for what had to be the hundredth time that morning.

"He's in a coma and yes, there is a possibility he won't come out of it," he explained in a blunt but sensitive tone.

"A coma, oh my God!" Katie cupped her hand over her mouth and began to tremble, as if the word coma was part of Zach's obituary.

"But then again," Dr. Kim continued, "he may wake up in an hour, a week, a month, we just can't say. He is actually quite fortunate to have survived at all."

A slight feeling of relief was apparent as she aggressively probed the surgeon for more information. "And if he does wake up, will he ever be normal again?"

Before he could answer, she swept her listless bangs from her forehead and added, "And please be completely honest with me Doctor."

"Again, Mrs. Bell, I cannot say for sure, but there is some hope for a full recovery, yes. But on the other hand, there could be permanent brain damage. Comas are tricky things to read and what happens in one case can be completely different from what happens in another."

Exhausted, Katie employed both arms to once again separate herself from the chair she had occupied for most of the previous seven hours. The tunnel vision that encapsulated Dr. Kim subsided and the waiting room fell back in around him. The steady buzz of morning rounds, present since the start of the 8 A.M. shift, invaded her ears for the first time.

"Can I see him?" she stooped down to retrieve her purse, which had been resting on the floor between her ankles.

Dr. Kim briefly shuffled her request in his head, then responded somewhat hesitantly, "Well ... I guess there would be no harm in that, but only for a few minutes."

He let out a small grunt as he rose up from his chair, communicating his own symptoms of fatigue, and then started past an empty coat tree toward an unattended desk identified by the sign above it as "VISITOR INFORMATION."

"Right this way," he instructed.

They rounded the corner to a lengthy hallway, guarded on either side by a series of doors through which the occasional orderly or nurse would emerge. Dr. Kim stopped at the beginning of the corridor and raised his right arm up from his side, extending a finger out in front of him. "Your husband is in 203B, four doors down on the right; I'll be down in a bit."

Katie offered her thanks before proceeding down the hall. She mumbled under her now thick and musty breath, silently reading off the black stenciled numbers on each door she passed, 200B ... 201B. The joints in her legs protested each step she took with a loud creak. A convoy of uneasiness trucked through her veins as she trudged heavily past a partially consumed breakfast on a white cart outside of 202B. She approached the door labeled 203B. Her frayed nerves tangled and her empty stomach gnawed at morsels of anxiety. All she had consumed over the last six hours was a bag of Doritos and half a can of Mountain Dew that she had purchased from the mall of vending machines in the waiting room. Turned out to be a good thing; however, because had there been anything substantial to throw up, she probably would have lost it at that moment.

She stopped for a few seconds and peered in through a small rectangular window above the doorknob, barely able to read the familiar terrain of her husband under light blue sheets on the bed across the room. Grasping the dull silver knob firmly, she summoned then released a deep breath that did little to calm, then pushed the door open and stepped inside the cool, uninviting confines of the room. She took a few steps and paused, barely noticing the undisturbed bed on her left. Her eyes inspected the entire length of Zach's frame and when they fixated on his pale expressionless face, she almost broke down, stumbling the final few paces to his bedside. The intricate array of tubes that spider-legged from various body parts and the wardrobe of elastic fiber that bandaged his shaved head and the lacerations on his face and arms; this version of her husband was almost too intolerable for Katie to accept.

She knelt down on the cold floor beside him, placing one hand gently on his shoulder and the other—the one clutching a pink tissue she had pulled from her shirt pocket—on the side of the mattress.

"Hey baby, it's me, it's Katie," she whispered, trying to stifle her tears as if he would somehow feed off any strength she might brandish. "The doctor says you're gonna be just fine," her voice quivered as the innocent untruth rolled off her tongue and a few tears trickled down her face. *Was it really a lie if he couldn't hear her?* It didn't matter anyway. She had to be positive. Positive thoughts breed positive results. "You've gotta get better, you've just gotta wake up and get better real soon, okay?" her words trailed off in yet another outbreak of weeping. She sniffled and brought the damp tissue up to her face, quickly regaining her composure. "The girls and I, we're counting on that."

Suddenly, a memo of the other woman flashed in Katie's head like a Post-It note tacked to her brain. Tempted by an abrupt twinge of resentment, she felt a strong urge to mention her, to ask Zach about her right then and there, even though she knew he wouldn't answer. She did not.

"Nothing negative," she reminded herself, tucking her suspicion into a deep dark drawer of thought and slamming it shut. "Wait until you see Aria in her Nala costume," she said, shifting her deliberations in a different direction. "She's just the cutest little lion princess ..."

Just then, the door behind her opened and that unwavering buzz pursued Dr. Kim into the room. Katie turned her head and glanced over her shoulder, picking him up out of the corner of her eye.

"Hangin' in there?" he inquired as the door shut behind him, once again sealing out the noise.

"Oh, Dr. Kim, you startled me." She pulled herself up off the floor and began to rub her hands in a circular motion on her kneecaps, a futile attempt to iron the numbness from them. "I guess I should probably be going now," she stated, sensing that the doctor was about to suggest the same.

"I don't mean to chase you out Mrs. Bell, it's just that we have to do some more tests, you understand."

Katie secured the leather strap of her purse on her right shoulder blade and adjusted it slightly for a more comfortable fit as she walked across the room. "Absolutely, but I would like to bring Dove and Aria to visit him later tonight, if that would be okay."

"Your daughters?" Dr. Kim inquired as Katie forced a half smile and nodded.

"That would be fine," he continued. "Evening visiting hours are six to nine. Until then, go home and try to get yourself some rest. I'll contact you immediately if there is any change in his condition."

Katie cast a final glance toward Zach's lifeless body, reeled for a moment in the dreadful image, then turned her weary eyes on Dr. Kim who now held a chart and stood at the foot of the bed. "Thank you so much for everything Dr Kim," she said as she struggled to pull open the heavy door. He bowed his head in acknowledgment before turning his attention back to the clipboard in his left hand. With that, Katie stepped out into the hall and into the buzz.

Chapter Six

It was 5:30 in the evening, nine hours after his surgery, when something wrestled Zach's soul from the deepest recesses of his coma. Voices ... mere whispers, and yet they rumbled like tremors when the earth swallows itself. "Zach, we're waiting for you."

He opened his eyes to the blurred silhouette of a nurse hanging dinner on the hook where lunch had been. As the image came into focus, he realized he was in a hospital.

"Did you say something? Nurse, are you talking to me?" the attractive middle-aged blonde tending to his IV did not even flinch as he spoke.

"Hey nurse ... hello, can you hear me?" She said nothing.

"Goddamn it lady, answer me!" his weak voice suddenly grew loud and demanding.

He sat upright in his bed as the nurse collected a clipboard and the empty IV bag from the stainless steel table to his right. Still, she did not react.

What in the hell was going on? Why was this ignorant bitch ignoring him? His mind started to swerve on wheels of confusion. And what was he doing in the hospital? There was no pain. He did not feel sick, not even the slightest discomfort. So why was he here? How did he get here? He tried to remember something, anything, but there were no memories of where he had been or what he had been doing in the hours leading up to now. Or, had it been days? Weeks? The last thing he had been doing, as far as he could recall, was downing another drink at the Reese party. Maybe that had something to do with where he was and why he could not remember getting there. He scanned the room for clues.

There was a vacant bed a few feet away, crisp sheets hugging the shape of the mattress like Saran Wrap. A nineteen-inch flat screen television was fastened to the wall by a V shaped bracket, suspended eight feet from the floor. Typical sallow hospital decor surrounded him but nothing to indicate why he was there.

"Zachary, we're waiting for you," the ominous voices, which he had dismissed as the final fleeting seconds of a nightmare he could not remember, returned. "We long to know the scent of your burning flesh ... and your rotting soul."

Quite startled, Zach once again searched the room, wall to wall, ceiling to floor, a curious eye seeking what he hoped would be some rational explanation. To Hell with why he was here. Where were those voices coming from? An eerie chill washed over him as he pulled his goose-bumped arms into his chest and hunched his shoulders nervously. The distorted serenade, drowned in the agony of those who beckoned, seemed to originate from every tiny, unseen crack and crevasse around him.

"Who the fuck are you?" he demanded, his fear turning to anger as if, for a brief moment, he had convinced himself that the whole thing was some sick practical joke. He even did a quick mental inventory of possible culprits who might be responsible, then listened intently for the voices to continue. They did not.

Barefoot and draped in a powder blue robe, Zach hoisted himself onto the cold floor and cautiously made his way across the room as another flock of goose bumps emerged from his chilled flesh. He walked about ten feet across the checkered linoleum before turning back toward the bed. What he saw just then arrested him with a fear he had never known before, a fear that ripped into common sense with the effortless ease of a liar's words through gullibility. This was no joke!

Himself. He saw himself, still lying there on the bed, his earthly existence dangling from the plastic fingers of life support equipment that maintained his being with a soft, rhythmic hum. He closed his eyes tight and desperately tried to squeeze the troubling illusion out through his pressed eyelids. But when he opened them again, the image of his listless self lying on the bed was still there, frozen in front of him. He seemed nothing more than a slab of meat on a giant platter. But how could this be?

Zach slowly retraced his steps back to the side of the bed. He stood there in a state of bewilderment, gazing down upon his vacant shell like the reflection in some misinformed mirror.

Was he dead? His mind grasped for whatever answers his suddenly fragile sanity might produce. A beating heart authored the lines on the heart monitor and every beep of life seemed to extract a little more balance from cogitation. But if he wasn't dead, what in the hell was going on? An answer came too quickly. "I must be going fucking crazy!" he reasoned aloud to himself, and then paused to process that suggestion. "No, this is all just a really bad dream. Very real, but just a dream."

He pried his focus from his comatose body and marshaled enough strength in his wobbly legs to walk back across the room and out into the hallway. Something wasn't right about this either. In fact, nothing about it was.

The abandoned corridor into which he stepped was not that of a modern, functioning hospital. There were weeds sprouting up through large cracks in the floor. Rats and roaches scurried across it as if they sensed an approaching flood. The white tile walls were covered in suet, dried blood and graffiti, and the arced ceilings, in an intricate maze of cobwebs. From the looks of it, the building had simply been forgotten. Except, he was here and he felt very profoundly that he wasn't alone.

He noticed a brown leather wheelchair lying toppled on its side. The chrome wheel closest to the ceiling spun slowly, around and around, producing a faint but steady "click ... click ... click."

Suddenly, the door to his room slammed shut behind him. Zach practically jumped out of the skin it seemed he had already abandoned, literally. His heart pummeled his chest feverishly as he struggled to recapture the oxygen that had temporarily fled his lungs. None of this made any sense. He felt normal. How could he be dead? Or was he? He still hadn't figured that one out yet.

He started to walk, completely baffled, past the overturned wheelchair and down the long stretch of hallway that led to an elevator some seventy five feet in front of him. Satanic messages were plastered across the walls to either side. "BLACK FOREST BABIES SWOLLEN WITH RABIES" and "LUCIFER IS THE ETERNAL KING."

There were drawings as well. Some were relatively simple and nondescript while others were quite elaborate and meticulously detailed, as if the disturbed artist had spent countless hours on them. There was an encircled pentagram surrounded by three Roman numerals. It appeared to be some type of a satanic clock with three of its five arms pointing to a different number … IX, I, III. Zach assumed they had some cloaked significance that he was unable to decipher.

Another drawing, significantly more detailed, depicted a man sitting upright against a mammoth tree. Its trunk and branches resembled the masculine torso and arms of a human male. The roots were serpents that had shot up through the earth and wrapped themselves around the man's wrists and ankles. Zach got lost for a moment in the disturbing images. Were they intended for his eyes?

He continued languidly down the corridor, weakened not by physical ailment, but rather, by the cancer of confused terror that spread throughout his insides. The foul stench of urine that thickened the already dense air had grown stronger and stung his nostrils.

What was this place? A hangout for rebellious teens who snorted cocaine from a Quiga Board? Perhaps a secret refuge for some satanic cult. Despite the steady departure of rational thought, Zach attempted to logically reason away what had become much too uncanny for his mind to accept. A nightmare. A figment of his imagination. That's what this place was. It had to be.

Suddenly, the screams of a woman penetrated the unsettling calm, shrieking unlike any he had ever heard. It came from a room several doors down on the right side of the hall. He wanted to turn and run in the opposite direction, away from the room. He couldn't. Like a cat being lured with a rubber mouse at the end of a string, he was being pulled closer and closer. He prepared himself for a ghastly, shocking sight, trying to subdue his fright by once again rationalizing that whatever was in there was just another part of the nightmare.

As he got only a few feet away, the screams became almost deafening and he could clearly make out the word "DELIVERY" written in fresh blood across the door that had swung open on its own. He also discovered that the woman, the one from whom the terrible screams originated, wasn't alone inside the room. He heard two other voices, male voices, shouting instructions to her in alternating bursts that mingled with the painful shrieks. "C'mon push, push. That's good, just keep pushing."

Zach was shrouded in curiosity, but still; he bartered desperately with the conscious world to extract him from this sinister fairy tale at once, to shake him awake before he got a glimpse of whoever was in the room. *Before they got a glimpse of him!* His pleas went ignored.

He now stood just behind the door that opened out into the hallway. His entire body was warm from the inside out and yet; he shivered reflexively against the chilled atmosphere. The screams continued to emanate from the room as he inhaled a deep, polluted breath, snaked his head around the door, and peered inside.

There was a birth in progress, the delivery of a child in the terminal stages. A beautiful gift from heaven above? No, this was no godsend, no miraculous occasion. It was in fact, something bizarre, something evil.

Zach's jaw dropped and the nerves of his right eyelid fluttered in objection as his wandering sight came to settle on the woman in the bed. For this woman, distended belly bared, legs propped up in stirrups two feet off the mattress, ankles shackled in leather buckles, was his mother, Anne. She was many years younger than the version he knew today but was still, without a doubt, his mother.

Erased by some chasm of misplaced time were the wrinkles that the passing years had gracefully etched into her face. Her graying hair was now gloss black and silk straight, as it had been some thirty years prior. He could vaguely remember her Cher-do from his days as a toddler and from the collection of silver framed memories displayed on a mantle at his parent's home above the fireplace, the one that had frightened him as a child.

To ensure that he and his brother Matthew wouldn't play too close to the hot sparks, Pop would scare them with tales of a viscous fire dog who would spring up from the smoldering ashes and bite their little noses if they got to close. "Feed the dog," he would say years later when he wanted one of the boys to throw a log on the fire. Even as an adult, when the family would make the three hour trek to Trenton for the holidays, Zach would sometimes catch himself gazing into the flames in search of the old crackling canine.

Speaking of his father Edward, he was there too. He wore Levi 501s and a tie-dyed shirt, and was about thirty pounds lighter in the gut than the guy who, during Thanksgiving dinner last November, ate so much turkey and candied sweet potatoes that he could hardly carry himself into the family room to watch the second half of the Steelers-Cowboys game. His hair was straggly and hung well past his shoulders. For a brief moment, Zach saw himself standing there, without the hippy hair and seventies garb, of course.

The reminiscing lasted only a few seconds before it retreated back into the rush of recurring horror that once again kidnapped his thoughts. This couldn't be happening, none of it.

As her pattern of heavy breathing was dissected by painful cries, now even more intense than before, Anne gathered every ounce of willpower she could muster and, at the request of the obstetrician perched on a three legged oak stool strategically positioned at the foot of the bed, gave it a single muscle-locking, lip-biting heave.

"Just one more and we'll be there," the doctor encouraged, fully aware that encouragement would be necessary to coax one last push. As a final, all-encompassing grunt followed a series of short, quick breaths and completely sucked up the last of Anne's energy, an explosion of stagnated cries burst into the air.

"Great job Annie," the doctor assured. "The baby's head is out."

Zach's vision stuck to the doctor's gloved hands like Superman on Silly Putty as they grasped the newborn's protruding head. With a gentle tug, the entire upper torso was extracted from the bleeding cavity through which it had just entered the world. Buzzing collaborated with crying as a swarm of horse flies gathered around the infant. Zach could taste the dry fear that coated his throat and the roof of his mouth as he swallowed. A second tug produced the entire form and the umbilical cord that still connected it to its former residence, now completely evacuated.

"Congratulations, it's a boy," the doctor announced as he held it up for the new mother to admire.

But it wasn't a boy, not a normal boy anyway. It appeared to be severely deformed, and when the doctor turned to allow Edward to examine his newborn son, Zach captured his first unobstructed view of the infant.

He was absolutely correct; it was grotesque. The head was unformed, incomplete. There were small indentations pressed into its soft skull, as if the demonic sculptor had only begun to press diligent fingers into the clay. Its pinkish skin was thin and semitransparent and allowed a view of its fresh organs—its beating heart and expanding lungs. And there were no lids to conceal the whites of eyes colored only by jutting streaks of blood red veins.

"You have the honor Dad," the doctor said as he handed Edward a pair of stainless steel surgical scissors and instructed him on precisely where to sever the umbilical cord.

"Thanks Doc," he replied as he took the instrument and proceeded to carefully snip the cord.

What was going on? Why was everybody so damned cheerful,

celebrating the birth of this hideous monster? Hadn't anyone noticed that this ... thing ... was not human.

The doctor raised the monstrosity high above his head as blood-tinted placenta dripped from it and collected in a puddle at his feet. "Thrust from a jackal's loin and regurgitated from the womb," he bellowed. "Oh unholy master, another of your kin has entered your world, spit unto this earthly misery."

Unholy master? Satan?

"Here, here," Edward praised as he lit up the dime store cigar he pulled from the pocket of his jeans. The doctor took the child, still covered in afterbirth, and placed it gently into the outstretched arms of its mother. "My precious little man," Anne cooed as she cradled the slime-soaked demon-baby near her breast.

Can't you see how disfigured it is? Zach wanted to yell out but dared not.

Anne began to sing as she rocked it back and forth in her arms. "Rock a by baby on the tree top ..."

Zach was quite dumbfounded and eminently horrified by the events that were unraveling before his eyes. Even nightmares had their limits.

Then, without warning, possibly disturbed by her choice of lullabies, the demon child swiped at Anne's face with its left hand, opening three deep gashes that extended from her right ear to the corner of her mouth. She only held it out away from her as it kicked and swatted at her bloody face. "No sweetie," she said in a calm maternal tone. "Be a good boy now."

"Sure is a rambunctious little fellow, ain't he?" Ed commented as he pulled a long drag from the cheap stogie and flicked the expended nicotine from its tip.

Three cuts in her face. Why only three?

Just then, Zach noticed something that had escaped prior scrutiny. The infant possessed only three fingers on each hand, six tiny appendages with six razor sharp claws, like the talons of a vulture.

As he vigorously shook his head back and forth trying to wake himself, Zach confiscated the attention of his mother for the first time. Smiling a devilish, crocked grin, she intercepted his glance. Then, she opened her mouth to speak.

"Mom?" Zach muttered with uncertainty before she could free the first words from her lips.

"Yes Zachary, it's me. It's just dear old mom."

"And dad?"

"Son," Edward acknowledged with a slight nod and an equally unsettling grin.

"Dad ... mom ... what the hell is going on?"

"Why, it's your birthday dear," Anne answered before Zach could finish the question.

Zach pondered this suggestion for a moment as confusion contorted his expression. "My birthday? Wait a minute, are you trying to tell me that thing is supposed to be me?"

"Supposed to be you?" Anne replied sarcastically, still holding the writhing abomination out in front of her. "But dear, it is you! And do you see the pain you've caused your poor mother already?" She pressed a finger to one of the gashes in her cheek before extending the blood-dampened tip out for Zach to observe. "You've been pretty good at that so far."

"Good at what?" Zach probed hesitantly.

His father answered for her. "At bringing pain to the women in your life."

Zach became defensive and, at the same time, chastised himself for speaking with people who weren't really there. Or were they? "You're fucking crazy! You're all fucking crazy! This whole thing is nuts and ... and well ... I'm certifiable!"

Zach had seen enough, and for the first time; he felt as if he could pry himself away from the room, as if the unseen fingers that had held him there for the past several minutes had finally relaxed their choke hold. He wrestled his vision from the unexplainable scene he had just witnessed and flung it down the hallway toward the elevator that was now approximately fifty feet away. He ran toward it as quickly as he could. Its open doors were inviting and seemed to provide an escape, a way out of this ... whatever it might be.

Chapter Seven

The way the clouds sometimes intercepted the rays of the sun before a late summer storm, stealing the shape from the shadows projected through the window onto the kitchen wall. The soothing jingle as seashell chimes danced lazily to the rhythm of a gentle breeze outside the screen door. The inviting aroma of Katie's homemade cinnamon-pecan pie. Everything about it was familiar to him. Zach was home. *But how?*

The elevator doors had parted and suddenly, there he was. For a while he stood motionless, restrained by confusion and fear, starring at Katie and the girls from the elevator car. He could see them, but they could not see him. It was as if he stood behind a two-way mirror. The doors of the elevator car remained open, open to the impossible visions that Zach tried to deny. Denial itself was nearly impossible.

Dove and Aria indulged themselves with pie and Kool Whip while mom gathered leftover hot sausage casserole and transferred it into a large plastic container. She took a roll of masking tape and a black marker from the drawer beside the sink and proceeded to label and date the container before placing it in the freezer. This was not normal post-dinner routine. Usually, Katie would place the food in a smaller microwave container and put it in the refrigerator for Zach to take to work the next morning. Nothing at this moment was normal, however.

Zach was losing his mind. Or, had he already lost it? None of this made sense. He was in a hospital just moments ago and now …

in his own house. It defied logic ... physics and yet, here he was. Could this all be a bad trip? Maybe that was it. Maybe someone at the Reese party had slipped something into his drink? Was it possible that he could still be at the party?

He stepped cautiously from the elevator into the kitchen, not totally surprised that his family was unaware of his presence. When he threw a glance back toward the elevator, it was gone. It was also apparent that Katie and the girls didn't miss him at all. He wasn't sure if there was reason to or not. Maybe they expected him home any minute. How was it they did not see him? Did not know he was already there?

Zach walked past the table where the girls gave each other whipped topping makeovers and stopped a few inches behind Katie, who wore her green and white striped apron as she loaded greasy utensils into the dishwasher. She turned quickly, as if she could sense that he was right there behind her. To his dismay, her attention had been summoned only by the mischievous goings-on at the table.

"Knock it off you two, you're making a giant mess over there." Katie looked right past him. Actually, she looked right through him.

"Aria started it," said a giggling Dove.

"Did not!"

"Did too!"

"Well, you're both gonna be cleaning up if you don't stop now!" The emphasis on the word "now" was quite effective as the food fight ceased immediately.

When the girls finished their pie, Katie collected their plates and tipped them over the wide mouth of the open waste basket, using a fork to chase the crumbs into its plastic tummy; then she strategically placed the final pieces into the puzzle that was the overloaded dishwasher. Zach only stood there, invisible, and watched. Watched and waited.

"Alright now, everybody into the living room," she instructed as she sealed the door on the dishwasher, started the presoak cycle with the push of a button, then grabbed a steaming Snoopy mug from the counter.

THE LOBBY 49

The now swirling winds, which over the past several minutes had whipped the soft ballad of chimes outside into more of a heavy metal concert, graduated into a full blown thunderstorm which rendered it just dark enough inside the house for lights.

As Zach followed his family into the living room, unnoticed, Katie pressed the small circular knob on the wall and turned it slightly, reducing the bright glare of the ceiling light to a subtle illuminated mist that allowed only the sharpest details of the room's country charm to perforate it.

Aria left the room for a moment and, when she returned; she was holding the camcorder her mom had used to record her school play. She plugged it directly into jacks on the front of the television as Katie settled on the sofa next to Dove. She pressed play on the tiny remote control before placing it on the oak coffee table next to her mother's steaming mug of herbal tea.

Aria parked herself on the sofa and, as she and her sister traded a few playful pokes, the Lion King suddenly dethroned a "Jack in the Box" who had just spilled the beans on another White House sex scandal. "Jack in the Box" was Dove's nickname for television news anchors.

"Too bad Daddy isn't here to watch me be Nala," Aria said.

"Maybe he's watching from Heaven." A trio of sinister snickers followed Dove's reply. Daddy wasn't laughing.

"I very much doubt that," Katie chuckled. "And besides, he never was much for keeping promises."

Zach, who stood completely unnoticed behind the sofa, quivered as an avalanche of unpleasant speculation, loosened by his family's disturbing dialogue, rumbled through his brain. Maybe this whole thing wasn't a dream. Maybe he *was* dead ... in limbo or something. Or worse yet, in Hell. The nightmare theory had certainly lost much of its earlier conviction. He had strung that idea out again and again and it was ready to snap. The whole thing was just too real to be a dream.

"I must be dead," he accepted. "That's it, I'm dead and they're laughing. But why are they laughing?" He spoke aloud and yet, only to himself. His tone grew furious. "Ha ha ha, they're having a good old time, just yukin it up."

Suddenly, Zach's thoughts were interrupted by Cukie Bird's seven o'clock squawk. Cukie Bird, as he was affectionately named, was the little wooden Cuckoo who lived in the little wooden house above the large wooden curio in the living room.

"Bye bye Cukie Bird," Aria called out just before the tweeting timepiece retreated back into the confines of his pine box chalet'.

Zach shifted his vision from the clock to the grand bay window that usually framed one of Mother Nature's many delicate and charming works of art. On the canvas of a lemonade horizon, the scene was truly a sight to behold. A robin's egg ribbon of Morning Glory sewn by the soil around a weathered white trellis and the trunk of a crimson-dyed Japanese Maple that, together with a stationary parade of Northern Pines, formed the organic skyline which sprawled the expansive front yard.

But on this evening, the backdrop was a mercury sky that had chugged down the lemonade and trampled out the splendor under a foot of lead-polished clouds. As Zach watched intently, mercury turned to black, black as thick as a moonless midnight. It was a shade of evening he had never seen before.

"Drugs," he tried to convince himself, "LSD. Someone had to have put some real potent shit in my drink."

The rain continued to batter the shingled rooftop above them and yet, Katie and the girls seemed as oblivious to the storm and to the eerie darkness that it spawned as they were to Zach's presence. Their focus had been claimed by the video of Aria's school play and only the chiming of the doorbell wrestled it away.

"I'll get it!" Dove announced anxiously as she and Aria simultaneously sprang from the sofa like a couple of real jack-in-the-boxes.

"No, I'll get it!"

Katie pressed the pause button on the remote as the two sisters raced across the room toward the front door. The bell sounded again and this time it was much louder, deafening in fact, but only to Zach's ears. He was overcome by a feeling of uneasiness as the bell echoed in his head. Somehow, whoever ... or whatever ... was at the door, knew he was there. Of that, he was certain.

Don't answer it, he wanted to shout but the words never formed into sound. Besides, he knew that, no matter how loud he screamed, he wouldn't be heard.

Aria opened the door as Dove struggled to reach the switch to turn on the porch light. "Can I help you?"

"Yes, can we help you?" Dove mocked as she played peek-a-boo behind her big sister's back.

Katie approached her daughters from the center of the living room. "Who is it girls?"

Suddenly, something occurred outside the doorway, something that Zach was unable to see from where he stood. Katie and the girls could see it; however, and soon the air was polluted with desperate screams.

Chapter Eight

Pain ... Zach recognized the feeling the instant it struck and even though it was more intense, more excruciating than any he had ever known, the familiar reality was welcome relief.

Darkness ... It was different now. No longer infinitely black and empty, the thin layer was contained only by closed eyelids that separated vision from light.

Screams ... Briefly distant, underwater muffled, then right on top of him again. They never ceased completely. They faded only for a moment and when they reemerged, the panic had been replaced by a positive excitement, the terror, by anticipation.

Dove and Aria hovered over Zach; he could smell the strawberry scented shampoo they used in their hair each morning. He shifted slightly in the bed, turning his head slowly to the left, then back to the right, then left again, as he let out a series of faint grunts.

"Doctor! Doctor! Somebody get Dr. Kim!" Katie called as she rushed out of the room and into the hallway, leaving her own feminine scent to hang in the air around him.

"Come on Daddy, please wake up." Dove's request was echoed by Aria.

Zach was awake and he knew it. He had come out of his coma, though he wasn't even aware that he had been in one. In fact, he wasn't sure where he had been or what had happened to him. He only knew that he was no longer *there*. He had escaped that awful nightmare.

A nightmare. That's all it had been.

Zach opened his eyes gradually and, as they adjusted to the crisp fluorescent light of the room, a comforting image came into focus above him. A greeting of cherry cheeks and pearly whites eased him gently back into the reality he had so desperately sought just moments ago. "Hi Daddy," Aria said with a smile as she leaned over him, a colorful candy necklace dangling from her neck only a few inches from his chin. He could not speak but was able to muster a reassuring wink and a half-smile.

His eyes found Dove next, seated beside her sister at the edge of the mattress. She giggled nervously. The sight of her father in this condition was something she didn't understand and, at her age; she wasn't sure how to handle it. She hadn't even recognized him at first, pale and lifeless, shaven head from surgery and gauze dressings covering much of his face.

Katie appeared at the bedside with an Asian man in white, a doctor. Her tear-dampened face added a bit to Dove's confusion. "These are good tears mommy's crying," she explained.

Dr. Kim's face held a puzzled, childlike expression, similar to the one that had just vanished from Dove's. He appeared in genuine surprise as he leaned over Zach and pressed a cold stethoscope to his chest. Although not impossible, such a quick emergence from a coma was rare, especially in a case as severe as this. "Hello there Zachary, it's nice to have you back," Dr. Kim said in a tone that suggested his disbelief.

Back from where? Zach wanted to ask but was unable to speak.

Just then, he remembered the accident. His mind began to tumble with the car as his final seconds of consciousness flickered like a movie trailer in his head. Even the severe trauma he had suffered did not erase the details of the mental videotape projected against his brain. In fact, his thoughts were quite sharp, as was the pain that shot through his entire mangled frame. His legs and arms felt sore and swollen. His ribs ached with each agonizing breath. And his head, it felt as if his skull had just been used as a wrecking ball.

"Do you recognize the woman standing behind me?" Dr. Kim probed, still holding the cold steel against Zach's breast. Katie smiled delicately and Zach shook his head ever so slightly to indicate that he did. "Good, very good," the doctor replied. "And how about the little ones?" Again Zach nodded a positive response as he grimaced in pain.

Dr. Kim stood erect as the stethoscope fell over his shirt collar. He walked a few paces to base of the bed, scribbled something on the chart that hung from the footboard, then started across the room toward the door.

"I'll give you all a few minutes to get reunited and then I'll need Zach for some tests and such. In the meantime," he continued from across the room, "I'll send the nurse down with something for that pain."

Zach gazed dryly up at his family. Even though it was difficult to think of anything other than the extreme discomfort that shot out through every nerve ending, it was equally difficult to forget the nightmare, especially that wall in the old, dilapidated hospital. Curiously, of all the horrible, sinister sights he had witnessed, it was that drawing of the encircled pentangle and the Roman numerals at three of its five points that was most vivid in his mind. IX, I, III. Nine, one, three. An omen perhaps? Nah!

Zach was never much of a believer in that nonsense, the prophetic power of dreams and all that other bull. Hell, he didn't even believe in Jesus Christ, or any other higher being or divine creator for that matter. Science, according to Zach, was the architect of all things. And as far as the architect of science itself? Well, he had never really given serious thought to that.

Besides, everything was fine now. His sudden revival had spared him and his family from whatever it was they had seen in the doorway right before he woke up—though he was certain that Katie and the girls were never truly in danger because they were never really there. And by the sound of their panicked tone, it was something hideous.

Katie took a seat on the bed between Dove and Aria and pulled them in close to her. Suddenly, thoughts of Judith Sample stirred inside her. The bastard had chosen a date with some bimbo over his daughter's school play. The urge to mention her surfaced once again, as it had during her first visit when Zach was still comatose. Once again that urge was swiftly suppressed with a false smile that forcefully lifted her cheeks. The time to deal with that matter would come, when Zach's condition stabilized, or at least when he was able to speak. Besides, it was probably just an innocent situation. She huffed inwardly. Who was she kidding? She hadn't thought that after the police had asked her if she knew the female passenger in the car. She certainly didn't believe it now.

Zach could suddenly sense that something wasn't sitting too well with his wife. Something was looting her peace of mind and somehow, he had a pretty strong notion of what it was. There was an obvious hint of tension in her eyes, a storm of anxious curiosity brewing in those seas of blue. It was indeed obvious, even in her attempt to conceal it.

Strangely enough, he could sense something else as well. Judith Sample was dead! Judith was dead and Katie, surely Katie knew about her. She had to know that someone else was in the car with him and that that someone was a woman. How could she not know? The police would have mentioned it. Especially if his feelings were accurate, if indeed, she hadn't survived the accident.

Like a scavenger that hovers cautiously over another's kill, he immediately began to pick at every fabrication that had ever saved a cheat from the wrath of the cheated in an attempt to salvage the perfect excuse. *She was just a friend and nothing more than that. We were carpooling. She was too drunk to drive her own car home.* He even rationalized that none of it was a total lie; just that it wasn't the complete truth. A devious mind tends to work that way. Even in his battered state, only moments removed from a life threatening coma, he scrambled for the alibi he knew, sooner or later, he would have to provide.

"Can we all go home now Daddy?" Dove asked.

Zach's weary gaze brushed past her and met Katie's. It was difficult for him to keep his eyes open and even more difficult to stare into his wife's while he silently deceived her.

"Not today sweetie, but pretty soon," Katie answered for him. "Daddy's got to stick around for a little while longer so they can take care of him."

As Katie turned toward Dove, Zach shut his eyes, as well as his mind. He was certain that he would have to deal with her curiosity, her jealousy. But he also knew that he had time; Katie would not confront him about Judith until he was well. And if the stench from his bullshit wasn't too pungent, he might even get out of it, just as he had before. And just as he had gotten out of that horrible nightmare.

* * *

11:02 A.M., the next day

Charlie Tuna never looked sorrier than he did suspended from the polyester confines of Larry Tesh's necktie. It was one of those "send $5.99 and three proofs of purchase" deals and nobody ate more Starkist than Larry. Tuna salad. Tuna casserole. Tuna tacos. In fact, his nickname down at the office was, fittingly enough, Tuna.

As he slouched in the naugahyde chair next to Zach's bed, Larry wondered if his friend was aware that Judith Sample had been killed in the accident, or if he was even aware of the accident at all. He had planned on telling him at some point, he just wasn't sure when, or how, to introduce it into the one-sided conversation.

"So, things are going really great with the Andromeda account. Your commercial for that shit man ... it's a huge hit." Larry tapped his fingers in awkward hesitation. "Everyone misses you down at the office ... well almost everyone. A few boneheads are blaming you for ..." Larry choked back the remainder of his sentence. He loosened the knot on his tie. "Too late dumb-ass!" he admonished himself under his breath. He had no choice but to tell Zach about Judith now. "I don't know if you heard but ..." Larry hesitated again to gather himself as a bead of sweat trickled over the creases in his forehead, "Judith didn't make it!"

Zach's glance never wavered. There was no surprise in his eyes nor, it seemed, any remorse. It was a stiff, disinterested response that gave Larry only a modest indication—Zach cocked his head slightly to look at his friend's face—that he was even heard at all.

Larry's relief was obvious, however. Maybe this was old news to his buddy and he hadn't been the first to break it to him. "The funeral is tomorrow at Parker & Sons over in Queens."

Zach was still and silent as Larry struggled inwardly to keep the conversation going and spin it back in a positive direction. "Hey man, but you, you are alive. And from what the doc is saying, there's a real good chance you're gonna come outta this thing showroom."

Zach didn't need any cheering up. He harbored little grief for his ex-mistress. In fact, he was somewhat relieved that there was one fewer voice that might reveal their little secret, might contradict whatever it was he would eventually tell Katie. The only thing he was going to miss about Judith was the convenience.

Larry leaned in close to Zach, as if the giant stuffed Saint Bernard he had brought as a get-well gift from the office was eavesdropping on the conversation. "I also heard that you were sauced as a worm in a bottle of Cuervo when you left that party," he said in a hushed tone that barely exceeded a whisper.

That was one little detail that Zach had forgotten and suddenly, dealing with his wife wasn't going to be such a big deal. At least not as big as dealing with the New York State Police.

"So tell me something," Larry barged in on his friend's escalating anxiety. "How come they didn't find any alcohol in your blood man, not a drop? You must have made some kinda deal with the devil or something."

What? No alcohol? But how? Just then, Zach remembered the image he saw right before he dozed off at the wheel, that disturbing satanic visage that appeared to him, that spoke to him. *A nightmare.* He had to keep reminding himself that that's all it had been.

The chair creaked loudly in relief as Larry lifted his large frame out of it. "Well bud, I'd better get going now. They need me to hold down the fort while you're away. Can't very well have both superstars out of the office for too long," he stated with a chuckle. Zach managed a half-smile as Larry headed for the door.

No alcohol. He rehashed the idea to himself as Larry lifted his arm in a departing gesture without looking back, and then vanished around the corner. Not even a drop? How could that be? Maybe the machine malfunctioned or they somehow mixed up the blood samples.

Although he wasn't sure how it was possible, he was elated that they hadn't discovered his intoxication. No intoxication would probably mean no charges against him; and we were talking about some pretty serious stuff ... DUI, Manslaughter ... Maybe, somehow, he really had made a deal with the devil.

Chapter Nine

Nearly a month had elapsed since Zach had been home, a long month that seemed like an eternity. If he hadn't been lucky, it could have been just that.

Few doctors are inclined to credit miracles over medicine and Dr. Kim certainly was not a member of that sparse group, but even he could not interpret Zach's recovery in terms of procedure or Penicillin. A patient is considered fortunate to come out of a coma at all, let alone in what could be measured in hours, and with no permanent brain damage whatsoever. Two minor scars, one on his forehead and the other across his left cheek, were all the physical evidence that remained of the accident.

While the fine doctor's handiwork had definitely played a major role in saving his life ... Zach suddenly remembered something Larry Tesh had said to him during his first visit to the hospital about "making a deal with the devil." He also remembered the nightmare he had while in the coma. Again!

"Strange," he muttered as Katie steered the silver Accord onto Crabtree Lane only a mile or so from home.

"What is it honey?" she inquired.

"What?" Zach blurted out in preoccupied delay.

"I thought you said something."

"Nope, just babbling to myself is all."

He labeled the whole issue "silly" and then purged it from his mind. "It's so nice to finally be going home. I was starting to get pretty sick of that damn hospital." Zach quickly changed the subject, one he certainly did not want to discuss with his wife. He smiled as he opened himself up to a place he hadn't been in quite some time.

The way the gravel of Crabtree Lane crackled like corn flakes beneath the car's tires. The sight of whitetail deer strolling the grassy backdrop of the Erricson's farm house. Even the scent of horse manure that emanated from the stables and fields behind the house was a welcome memory. Good old country living. Zach had to learn the finer details of home all over again. He also learned something else as Katie's car proceeded past the Erricson's driveway; two orange sheets, sewn together and strategically placed over a 76 V.W Beetle, can result in a pretty ghastly Halloween decoration.

The sun had just ducked behind the horizon as the Accord pulled into the driveway and Zach could see three tiny faces peering out around the curtains that dressed the large bay window of the living room. Dove and Aria waved with excitement as Mojo wedged himself between them, wagging his stump and barking anxiously at the approaching car.

He really was home and, even though his senses were somewhat numb from the pills that rendered excruciating pain bearable, Zach felt better than he had in a long time. That hospital room had been his prison far too long—its dreary blue walls closing in around him, tighter and tighter each day, various tubes holding him to his bed like shackles.

During the final two weeks of his dreaded incarceration, he had been allowed one half hour of "outside time" each afternoon, which he had usually spent with Katie, and sometimes the girls too, in a wheelchair behind St. Margaret's. He never had been able to breath in enough fresh air during that time to clear his sinuses. His lungs were still caked with the resin of heavy-duty air freshener and extra strength disinfectant that had been constant in his room.

Katie pressed the button on the remote clipped to the sun visor above her head and the garage door lifted slowly. The absence of his

THE LOBBY

Lexus in its customary spot next to the one Katie's Accord slipped into instantly reminded Zach why he had been away so long. A feeling of uneasiness came over him as he opened the passenger's door without caution and it swung freely until its hinges caught hold and jerked it back toward him.

"Hold on a minute dear," Katie instructed as she quickly climbed out from behind the steering wheel. "Let me help you out of the car."

Zach was still quite weak and Dr. Kim had advised him not to move around without support for at least another week. Katie came around to the passenger door and interlocked her arm with his. She yanked him upright so hard he had to grab hold of the car door to keep from tumbling on top of her.

"Gosh Kate, you trying to steal my arm or something?"

"Sorry dear, guess I don't realize my own strength."

As Katie helped Zach across the vacant concrete that was his parking spot, Dove and Aria appeared, stocking feet, at the doorway that led from the garage to the kitchen.

"Hi daddy," Aria said with a wide, chocolate covered grin that could hide neither her excitement nor the Double Fudge ice cream her and her sister had been enjoying.

"Daddy's home! Daddy's home!" Dove added as they scurried to him.

Zach pulled his arm out of Katie's and took a few steps forward. "Hi baby dolls," he said as he stooped cautiously to embrace them.

"Be careful," Katie warned. "Daddy's still pretty weak."

Just then, Pamela Logan stepped through the doorway and into the garage. Pam, Katie's big sister, had been watching the girls while Katie went to pick Zach up from the hospital. She was four years older and thirty pounds heavier than Katie, but still possessed that natural beauty and charm that seemed to characterize all the Solomon women. Good looks really did grow on trees, at least the Solomon family tree. "Welcome home Zach," Pam offered in a raspy voice that insinuated her affinity for nicotine.

"Thanks Pammy, it's damn good to be here!"

Dove and Aria led the charge as Pam and Katie helped Zach up the stairs and into the kitchen. They lowered him slowly into a chair at the table where the girls had resumed their attack on what was now Double Fudge soup. He left out a deep sigh as he scanned a place he had not seen for weeks.

"Well, I guess I'd better be getting home," Pam stated as she gathered her keys and purse from the counter. "Devil's Night starts a month early in our neighborhood and if one of those dirty little you-know-what's eggs the house and I'm not there, Harold will chase em down the street with his twelve gauge."

"Hey, thanks a bunch for watching these little rascals," Katie said as the girls giggled and Mojo begged for whatever it was in their bowls.

"Yes, thank you," Zach added.

"No problem ... Oh, by the way, a Lieutenant Pete something-or-other called for Zach earlier. I left his number on the counter. He said he'd be there till nine."

"Must be about the accident," Zach assumed as he glanced down at his watch and saw that it was only a quarter after six.

"Get plenty of rest and drink lots of your wife's herbal tea," Pam shouted back to him as she and Katie walked through the living room toward the front door. "It always does me a world of good."

He did not respond.

A sudden restlessness had begun to stir inside of him, restlessness about that phone call from the police. Dove and Aria pushed their empty bowls out in front of them as they got up from the table. They hugged their father in turn before scampering out of the kitchen, Mojo at their heels.

"Nothing to get all worked up about," he reasoned aloud to the empty room as he labored over to the counter in search of the number. He would have left that hospital in handcuffs had they known how much alcohol he had consumed that night. Besides, Larry had told him the police found no alcohol in his blood. Larry would never joke around about something like that, would he?

Still, Zach wondered if maybe, somehow, they had found out the truth … found out that he had been plastered on the night of the accident. Maybe his so-called "deal with the devil" was suddenly null and void. He struggled to balance himself against the counter as the sound of a firing ignition and the glare of headlights coated the air.

"So long, be careful." The shouted exchange of "good-byes" was barely audible above the clamor of Pam's 78 Monte Carlo, which pleaded for a tune up or, better yet, a junk yard retirement.

By the time the "clank" of the screen door announced Katie's return to the interior of the house, Zach had located the number Pam had scribbled next to Ed McMahon's cheesy mug on the official Publisher's Clearinghouse Sweepstakes entry. He was not the least bit aroused by the fact that he may already be the winner of Ten Million Dollars. He was, however, extremely concerned about the phone call from the police.

Lieutenant Pete Wolfe, 555-4000.

Katie walked back into the kitchen as Zach struggled to remember the location of the telephone. It had definitely been a while since he made a call from home and the pain pills did nothing to sharpen his mental map of the house's layout.

"I found the number," he informed her as she set the girl's ice cream bowls in the sink.

"Do you want me to call?" Katie offered.

"That's alright, I'll call." Zach absolutely did not want her to call. Talk to the police about the accident, possibly about Judith? *No way.* And what if they had found out about him drinking that night? If she found out?

"Okay, well I'm gonna go upstairs and check on the girls then. You should get some rest," Katie advised.

"I'll go in and relax on the sofa after I call this guy," Zach said, remembering that the phone hung on the wall by the microwave.

Katie's voice trailed off as she disappeared from the kitchen, "I'll bring you a pillow when I come back down."

He did not hear her. By now he had turned all of his attention to the business at hand. Damned cop! What the hell did he want?

Zach picked up the phone and dialed the number on the envelope. He almost hung up after the second ring but knew that avoiding the police could only make matters worse. Besides, they probably had his number traced on the first ring and would automatically return the call. How would he explain hanging up?

"State police," a rugged male voice answered after the fourth ring.

"Yes, may I please speak with a ... Lieutenant Pete Wolfe?" Zach requested hesitantly.

"This is Wolfe, how can I help you?"

Zach swallowed nervously, as if the mere mention of his name would instruct the officer to reach through the phone line and slap the steel bracelets around his wrists.

"My name is Zachary Bell, I got a message that you called earlier." Zach swallowed again and this time it was so loud he feared the lieutenant might detect his anxiety.

"Oh, yes, Mr. Bell, how are you doing? I understand you were just released from Saint Margaret's."

"Pretty well considering."

"You must be thrilled to be home. I spent a few days in that dump last April when I took some lead in the ass. Place is so damn depressing."

So far, so good. Now just get to the point. Zach fidgeted skittishly with the dangling phone cord as the idle chatter concluded.

"Anyway, the reason I called ..." a voice in the background pulled Wolfe away momentarily.

"C'mon, spit it out," Zach muttered under the hollow hush of Wolfe's hand veiling the phone.

"Sorry bout that," the lieutenant resumed. "We need you to come down to the barracks to ... excuse me." It was that annoying pest in the background again.

Come down? To what? Turn himself in? Answer some questions?

Take a Breathalyzer test? No, that didn't make any sense. What good would that do? Zach's mind was in a dizzying spin that was only partially the result of the painkillers he had taken three hours prior.

"Sorry again," Wolfe returned after several agonizing moments. "Like I was saying, we need you to stop by the station. We have some of your personal effects we recovered from your Lexus. A tool box, flares, some CDs, a pair of leather driving gloves and forty-six cents."

Relief.

"Whew, thank goodness that's ..." Zach's clumsy words stumbled into awkward silence, suspicious silence. He caught them just before they spilled too much. He was normally much more alert and careful when he spoke, but the Perks and drowsiness dulled his prudence significantly.

"Go on," the lieutenant probed in an almost interrogative tongue. "I'm still here."

"Oh, ah ..." Zach scrambled, "... the gloves, they were a gift from my girls, the first thing they ever bought me with their own money, you know, very sentimental."

"Of course, and the forty-six cents, I'm sure you really miss that too," Wolfe said in sarcastic laughter that suggested he was no longer curious about Zach's near blunder. Zach laughed too, more out of relief than humor.

"You can pick this stuff up here at the barracks," Wolfe instructed, "Monday through Thursday from seven till four. We'll hold it for thirty days."

"Thanks, I'll do exactly that."

"You know where we're located, right off the Turnpike, Exit 5 B?"

"I know right where you're at." Zach had no idea where Wolfe meant; but he wanted desperately to get off the phone.

"Alrighty Mr. Bell, you take care."

"I will, good night."

"Good night." Zach hurriedly slammed the receiver back into the cradle. He badgered himself for being so stupid, then commended himself for the almost instantaneous recovery.

The police had no reason to suspect him after all. They had no evidence against him; they had found no alcohol in his system, even though they should have. Still, Zach was surprised that they didn't even wish to question him about the accident at all. They had apparently already ruled it just that ... an accident. His deal with the devil hadn't fallen through.

Chapter Ten

A match was struck and an image of the Virgin Mary was revealed, painted in delicate tones on hundreds of individual tiles that formed the mosaic on the vaulted ceiling high above. Her gentle eyes gazed down upon him in sorrow and the surrounding angels seemed to be trying to console her.

Candles were lit by a young boy in a white robe soiled with dirt and blood. Their brilliant flames swallowed the darkness like a mammoth bonfire. The smell of incense sweetened the air and filled his lungs with every desperate gasp.

A congregation of ordinary faces, women and children, fathers and grandfathers, stared at him from the rows of mahogany pews occupied from end to end. All were strangers, silent and attentive, like a courtroom jury.

Somehow, Zach was in a church now. It was St. Luke's, the church where he and Katie had been married and where Dove and Aria had been baptized. He hadn't been here for nearly six years, but he recognized it without hesitation.

He sat naked and elevated nearly six feet off the ground, on an unusually tall wooden chair next to a free standing alter canopied under a baldachin of marble and draped in red silk. On the altar sat a black book. It appeared to be some type of a bible, though it certainly wasn't holy. A picture of a goat's head was etched into its cover and he could make out the words "RITES OF DARKNESS" through the dust and cobwebs that had only recently been disturbed.

Zach felt groggy, as if he had just awakened from ... or into ... a dream. Another nightmare. Or was it?

He was able to feel the burning bite of barbed wire that held him in place on his unholy throne. The wire snaked around his arms, holding them flat against the chair's unfinished planks. It was also entangled around his ankles and the legs of the chair that extended to the floor below his bare feet. The feeling was very real. Nightmares weren't supposed to be real.

Zach's gaze was heavy as the cathedral's spectacular detail came in and out of focus. Intricate patterns of stained glass and etched marble filtered in pieces through his distorted vision. The gothic size of the nave and the Romanesque heaviness of its walls was ever present around him and he could feel it with his eyes closed. This had to be a dream. Then he winced in pain as the barbed wire burrowed deeper into his flesh.

Suddenly, a deep, sullen voice called out from behind him, "All rise." Zach turned to identify the speaker but, for the moment, was able to make out only an anonymous black figure standing beside the cathedral's screened choir stall, a filigree of white stone and gold accents. When he heard the disturbed shuffle of rising bodies, he looked back out upon the members of the congregation who had been staring at him from the pews. All of them were now standing and their heads were twisted away from the altar, as if their necks had been broken. All but one. Was that Katie still facing him from the back row? Zach squinted as the fear inside him expanded until it felt as if it would burst through his throbbing veins. *It was Katie.*

A priest stepped out from behind him and into the unusually radiant light of the candles. Zach shifted his vision slightly and immediately recognized the elderly gentleman who now stood before him, cloaked in a black robe with red sash and red cuffs. "Father Kazcmarek?"

The silver-topped man in the black robe nodded. "You remember me?"

Zach knew only one priest. The one who had married he and

Katie. The one who had baptized Dove and Aria only because Katie insisted that they get a little exposure to her religion.

"Of course!" Zach explained, finding momentary relief in the priest's familiarity. "You married me and Katie and baptized my little girls."

"Oh yes, Dove and Aria, sweet little things indeed," the old man closed his eyes and traced his upper lip with his tongue. "If only we had been alone."

Zach was puzzled by Kazcmarek's words. "What do you mean?"

"Aria was the one that really whet my appetite and Dove, precious Dove."

Zach turned his focus forward. The congregation was now seated and facing him once again. Everyone except Katie. She stood at the far end of the aisle that split the pews, and the church, down the middle. Wearing her wedding gown and clutching a bridal bouquet of wilted roses, she shuffled with deliberate steps down the aisle toward him. He struggled against the jagged restraints that bound his wrists but they only tightened, cutting further into his skin as he tried to free himself. And he struggled against the terror, terror that threatened to suffocate him from the inside.

"There is little sense in struggling," Father Kazcmarek offered. "They have already come for you, just as they had come for me."

"Come for me?" Zach questioned as he glanced over to the priest. "Who's come for me?"

The priest continued, ignoring Zach's question, "It got so horrible that I just caved in." The old man turned his attention back toward the attentive congregation, their morbid expressions sustained in the exotic dance of flickering fire. "I snapped my own neck like peanut brittle and just gave myself to them."

Zach gazed back out at Katie. She now stood only a few feet from where he sat. He could make out the tear that trickled down her soft cheek. He could also see the wicked curl form at the edges of her mouth as her expression turned from one of melancholy to uncanny amusement.

Zach tugged on the barbed wire once more and once more the burning sting immobilized him. "Father," he called through the pain, hoping that his past association with the priest would invoke sympathy and, possibly, a logical answer from the old man. "What is this? What is going on? Why am I having these awful nightmares?"

"Nightmares … I'm afraid not. Although, that is exactly what I thought too, at least in the beginning."

Zach shook his head, "I don't understand."

The priest again turned his attention away from Zach and took a few deliberate steps toward the congregation. "You see," he started, addressing both Zach and those seated in the pews, "the children were my weakness. I gave my life to Jesus but the children are the reason that Satan took it instead. I was weak and succumbed to his temptations, just as this young man has done. I wore the Son of God around my neck, but not in my heart." Kazcmarek turned and walked to Zach. "I just couldn't refrain from sin and neither could you. That is why we will both burn in hell … eternally. Mine was most unforgivable but yours … well; let's just say that your lack of faith has sealed your fate." The priest peered upward. "Unlike you, I never doubted God's existence, not for a moment. I suppose I just believed that his mercy was limitless, even for someone as vile as myself."

Zach closed his eyes tight and began to shake his head vigorously. "Alright, time to wake up. Just wake up."

"Silence you fool!" Kazcmarek bellowed before calming to a near whisper. "There is nothing you can do. God does exist and he has spoken. Oh, his wrath is silent at first, a storm without thunder," the old man's voice began to rumble once more. "But when the skies open up above you, that's when Satan comes to give you shelter in a sanctuary of eternal suffering." Kazcmarek's voice softened once again, "The rain has already begun to fall on you, Zachary Bell."

Zach's eyes opened and his sight shifted away from Kazcmarek. He noticed that Katie was gone. There was, however, something else emerging to harass him. A child of six or seven appeared from behind. Then another. And another. Nine in all, six boys and three girls, assembled in a random cluster around the chair. They were robed in soiled white cloth, just like the one who had lit the candles and brought Zach into this terror. Their faces were pale and their lips had been stitched shut. One of the children, a boy, glanced up at Zach as the priest came to his side. His eyes were gray and lifeless, without hope or expression. The others were just like him.

"This was my obsession ... my damnation," Kazcmarek said as he placed a caressing hand on the boy's left shoulder. He took a deep breath through his nostrils, then pulled the hand back down to his hip. He peered up at Zach, eyebrows set in scrutinizing thought, "Take him!"

Zach's fear simmered as the colossal church began to rumble and the tiles of the Virgin Mary mosaic that seemed to cast pity upon him earlier, dropped from the ceiling, pelting him like hail. The barbed wire that fastened him to the chair began to rust, as if months, along with Zach's sanity, were being consumed by each passing second.

Suddenly, acting upon the priest's direction, the children moved in closer to Zach. They were only children, but then again ... what were they going to do to him as he sat there, helpless, defenseless? With the strength of adult men, four of the tiny soldiers began to lift the chair off the floor. "Hey!" Zach cried. "What are you doing? Please, don't listen to him."

"It is not really me to whom they listen," Kazcmarek stated as the children continued to execute their duties.

"Please, please ..."

The children carried the chair, and Zach, past the altar and toward the opposite side of the church. They hauled him fifteen feet or so, then dropped the chair down with such force, he was certain it would collapse beneath him.

He grimaced against the intensifying pain in his wrists and ankles; the jagged spikes of the barbed wire restraints dug deeper into the skin, rubbing against raw bone. But what he felt more than anything else was the fear. *I'm going to die!* Even if this is just a dream, I'm gonna have a heart attack in my sleep or something.

He felt faint and silently pleaded for that reprieve. It never came. Something else did though, something that rocked him with grim familiarity. *To his right, laughter.* And not just any laughter.

"Dove?" his voice quivered as he turned toward the sound. "Aria, is that you?" *Laughter in front of him now.* He swung his head forward again. His daughters stood at his feet. They were not wearing white robes like the other children. Dove wore a purple dress, Aria was in pink. Nor were their mouths stitched shut. They were not, however, the daughters that Zach knew.

It was in their eyes, tiny crimson pupils in deep pools of onyx. It was pure evil. Not something with which they had been born, but rather, something they had acquired. From the priest? Zach wasn't sure. All he knew, all he was certain of, was that the wickedness in his daughters' eyes, the hatred … it was meant for *him*. He could feel it throbbing in his temples. Or, was that the rush of blood?

Dove moved slowly toward him and Aria followed. The other children gathered around like leopard cubs waiting for their turn at the kill. What were his little darlings going to do to him, and why? They each placed a delicate hand on one trembling knee. Then, with a soft, simultaneous grunt, they pushed.

Kazcmarek began to chant, "Fallen angel, become the flame." Somehow, the priest's words registered in his scrambled thoughts as the chair teetered for a few deliberate moments on its hind legs. Zach leaned forward in a desperate attempt to stop it from falling. He winced and braced his neck as he realized his attempt was futile. The back of the chair, and the back of his head, slammed against the hard floor. It felt as if the blunt impact cracked open his skull. Still, he did not lose consciousness. "Fallen from grace, in his name."

Dove and Aria stood over him, gazing down into his watery eyes. "Please babies, don't hurt Daddy," Zach pleaded through the foggy swirl of agony.

"But Daddy," Dove said in tepid retort, "you're just a worm and were gonna do you a favor and put you back in the ground with all the other slimy creatures."

"Deep in the ground, where all the yuckie stuff is at," added Aria, her eyes now aglow in wild, radiant hostility.

Both girls knelt down in the puddle of blood that drained from either side of their father's head. They opened their hands, stretching their tiny fingers apart just above his face. For a brief moment, Zach noticed something beyond their hovering bodies.

The entire church, as much as he could see of it anyway, was completely engulfed in flames. A searing heat, seemingly gathered from the inferno that encapsulated them, emanated from the tips of his daughters' fingers. As they lowered their hands toward his face, he felt the singe of his eyebrows and the smolder of skin on his forehead. "Nooooo," he squealed as he squeezed his eyes tightly shut against the molten pain.

Then, all at once, the heat was gone. Zach felt the touch of Aria's hand on his left shoulder. It didn't burn. There was no pain at all. She shook him and said something he couldn't make out. He opened his eyes and saw her leaning over him. He turned his head to the right and saw Dove as well. She was in her pajamas, bouncing up and down, her knees pressing into the mattress a few inches from his head. "Come on Daddy, wake up!

Wake up?

"Yeah Daddy, wake up, it's time for breakfast."

Zach was awake … and in his very own bed.

Chapter Eleven

"Kayser ... Kazakos ... Kazar ... Kazcmarek .... . Kazcmarek." Zach mumbled to himself as the index finger of his right hand came to a halt near the bottom of page one thousand and one. *Kazcmarek.*

It was 9:32 in the morning and Zach sat hunched over the kitchen table. An untouched glass of orange juice and the world's thickest paperback, the New York Metropolitan Area White Pages, tarnished the otherwise restaurant crisp arrangement of floral place mats.

There were more names between the covers of the city directory than he could fathom, but Zach searched for only one, frantically. A bead of sweat trickled down his forehead even though the brisk morning seeped through the screen door into the kitchen.

He had to find the number of Father Kazcmarek and speak with him directly. No, he didn't even want to speak with him. He just wanted to hear the old man answer the telephone, hear his voice, the voice of a living, breathing human being. That would confirm that his dream was exactly that, just a dream.

"Adam ... Andrew ... Angelo ... Beatrice ... Bernard. There he is, Father Bernard Kazcmarek, 202 Filmore Street, 498-8916."

Zach didn't waste time jotting the number down; he circled it before ripping the entire page from the book. With over seven thousand pages, who would miss it anyway?

He took a swig of orange juice and then jumped up from the table, tripping over Mojo who, until that moment, had found the linoleum at Zach's feet a reasonably comfortable spot for grinding on pig's ear. "Damn it Mo, get outta the way," Zach cursed as he regained his balance.

The moody Jack Russell returned a few indecencies in grumbled, low pitch dog-speak, then collected the gnawed treat in his jaw and settled into an equally suitable location under the table.

Katie had taken the girls to school before her nine o'clock pedicure at Beverly's Boutique, so Zach was alone in the house. That was, except for the disinterested Terrier who had already resumed his daily regimen of dental hygiene among the sanctuary of finely crafted oak.

Zach shuffled to the phone and fumbled the instrument as he impatiently snagged it from its cradle. He got a firm grasp on the receiver and began to rapidly push buttons as he recited the number he had circled. Shit! He hit the 7 instead of the 8. He hung up and started over, pressing each digit in agitated certainty as he announced them sarcastically. When the correct number was punched, he pulled the receiver up to his ear and listened.

The first ring seemed unusually loud and drawn out. The second was even more pronounced. Zach tapped his left foot in nervous anticipation as it faded almost seamlessly into the third. "C'mon, answer the damned phone."

"Hello," a grandmotherly voice abruptly choked off the sixth ring, just as he was about to hang up.

"Hi, may I please speak to Father Bernard Kazcmarek."

There was a lengthy pause at the other end of the line; a hollow silence that somehow told Zach he had just said something wrong. When the silence finally cracked, the sweet voice on the other end was now sharp and resentful. "Is this some kinda joke?"

"Oh no ma'am, I'm a former ... well, let's just say my family ..."

"He's not here," the woman angrily interrupted, obviously choked up by what she assumed a prank.

"Well, when do you ..." the terse response of a loud bang caused Zach to yank the phone from his ear and the dial tone that followed was audible long before he pulled it back.

He slowly reached to hang up the phone, missing the cradle on the initial attempt as he stared down at the floor. A feeling of uneasiness stirred a minor quake in his gut.

Did this confirm the minister's passing? Was Father Kazcmarek really dead, just as Zach had dreamt? Had the priest really taken his own life in such a violent manner? And if so, how could Zach have known? He hadn't been to St. Luke's, or any church for that matter, since Dove's baptism. He hadn't read or heard anything about any suicide. So how could he have dreamt about it? Was the nightmare some type of a premonition? An omen?

Zach had wondered the same thing about the dream he had while in the hospital. But this one was different somehow. He was convinced for a moment that he had actually felt pain, real pain, and not just a sting from the old pinch test either. He remembered the barbed wires digging into his flesh as he glanced down at his wrists, turning them in thorough inspection. *Nothing.* Of course it had been a dream. He chuckled, lending a false sense of conviction to his thoughts.

Still, Zach had to know more about Kazcmarek. He had to know if the priest was in fact, dead. He had to know if he had really killed himself. The old woman on the phone, probably one of Kazcmarek's former parishioners, had sounded as if Zach were completely out of line asking to speak with him. She sounded like an irate widow, even though Zach was pretty sure that Roman Catholic priests weren't permitted to marry. But had the old man really committed suicide? Zach needed answers.

Chapter Twelve

(New York Times, Monday, September 28, 2002 edition, front page)

"ADMITTED CHILD MOLESTER FOUND DEAD"

A former Catholic Minister, who was sentenced to a minimum of nine years for child molestation, was found dead in his cell by a guard during routine rounds early Saturday morning at the Quinville Mental Institution in New York.

Bernard Kazcmarek, 62, the victim of an apparent suicide, was found by guard Ellis Fitzsimmons, 34, of Yonkers.

Kazcmarek was a priest at St. Luke's Church in Mt. Vernon, which burnt to the ground in July in an apparent act of revenge, possibly carried out by angry parents. The suspected arson occurred only days after charges of child molestation were filed against Kazcmarek. He is believed to have broken his own neck in a manner too horrific to describe in detail.

A disturbing suicide note was written on the wall of the cell in what police are saying was blood from the mutilated middle and index fingers of his right hand. The gruesome discovery, under investigation by police and the city coroner's office, has police and hospital officials alike extremely shaken.

"It was like something out of a horror movie," Fitzsimmons said in a deposition taken by police at the scene.

Nineteen prior suicides have occurred at the hospital for the criminally insane since it opened in 1962, but officials are saying that this was by far the most unsettling.

"Seeing stuff like this is part of the job but it's nothing any of us will ever get used to," explained Lt. James Powell, 51, of the New York State Police. "It's certainly not going to be easy sleeping for a while."

Officials at Quinville described Kazcmarek, who had spent only two days at the facility before his death, as "extremely disturbed and delusional from the moment he arrived."

Fitzsimmons, an employee of the hospital for three years, stated that Kazcmarek was "particularly agitated earlier that evening" but stated that the patient had "calmed down considerably by lights out around 9:00 P.M."

"The old man was hysterical, like he'd seen a ghost or something," recalled Ross Kaufmann, 26, another guard on duty that evening. "I mean this fellow was truly convinced that the Boogie Man was going to get him, the way he was carrying on and all."

Kazcmarek, who pled guilty to fourteen counts of child molestation, was the priest at St. Luke's for nearly a decade and admitted to "improper sexual conduct" with alter boys and girls over a period of fifteen months from February 2001 through May of this year.

The parents of an 11-year old boy notified police after the boy told them of "games" that Kazcmarek would play with children at the church as well as at the priest's home in New Rochelle. Thirteen other children, all between the ages of 7 and 13, were interviewed, and nine of those children reported similar activity.

Kazcmarek was arrested on July 12 and never denied the allegations against him. It was shortly after that arrest that police say he became delusional; claiming that he was being "harassed by demons" who he believed had "come to claim my soul."

Although many believe that the stories were merely an attempt by Kazcmarek to avoid prison incarceration, psychiatrists testified that the priest was under "extreme mental stress" and may truly have been under the impression he was being pursued by something of a supernatural *nature. Judge Forrest Wasson ruled that Kazcmarek was "legally insane" and sentenced him to Quinville this past Thursday.*

Kazcmarek's body was transported to the New York City Coroner's Office early yesterday morning where a thorough investigation is being conducted. Police haven't ruled out anything yet, but consider foul play to be "extremely improbable" at this time.

* * *

Zach had been in the den for nearly an hour, browsing the Internet in search of something he hoped he'd never find. But there it was, framed neatly within the confines of the computer screen. The article's conviction swelled with each line and Zach didn't have to read between those lines to realize that the dream meant something.

Kazcmarek was, in fact, dead. And the children, this sick pervert of the cloth really had done things with them. Unimaginable things. Evil things. He was certain, however, that the priest had never done anything to Dove or Aria because they had never been alone with him.

Zach hadn't known anything of the minister's sordid past, or of his horrific passing. It was the dream that had told him everything he knew, everything that he had just verified in the old news article.

Was Kazcmarek trying to warn him of some impending peril? The message seemed more a threat than a warning, and it was becoming increasingly more arduous to dismiss it, or the other experiences for that matter, as a mere dream.

"But that really is all they were, just dreams," Zach mumbled to himself as he clicked the arrow on CLOSE and the deep blue screen absorbed the outdated news back into its memory.

He probably had read something about Kazcmarek before and just forgot. Or, maybe he had heard it on the news without really paying attention. The television could have been on while he was doing something else. The subconscious mind is like a sponge and these nightmares were ringing out all of its filthy water.

Zach had satisfied his suspicions, at least for the moment, but not without substantial coaxing. He even managed a chuckle as he turned off the computer and pulled himself away from the desk on which it sat. He convinced himself that the news about the priest was something he had known about all along and didn't even realize it until now. He shook his head as he walked out of the den. He knew something else as well. He really wanted these nightmares to stop.

Chapter Thirteen

Two weeks later

Neon nights, white lights, like eyes, back and forth, spotlights, seeking dreams to waste. The invitation of "LIVE NUDES" and "EROTIC MASSAGE" flickered purple and green through the envelope of chilled autumn air as a parade of headlights weaved a seam through the fabric of the city.

East-enders, West-enders, Uptown clowns with plastic wealth and pregnant egos, the last remnants of nine to five New York looked to escape the nocturnal routine that had settled in.

Vendors of the evening, daughters and sisters under the stars, selling false love and fifty dollar dignity, toxic sex. It was a typical New York night on the rocks, definitely shaken, not stirred.

Zach sat at the window of his studio office, forty-two stories above the shuffle of those who were either hurried to the sanctuary of a topless joint by the fear of the ever-present criminal element, or slowed by whiskey and the absence of any particular place to be.

He had only been back a few days and already he had a deadline staring him in the mug. It was Thursday and his presentation to the dairy reps was set for Tuesday morning. He gazed aimlessly out across the city's endless skyline, over glistening silver soldiers of glass and steel, hoping to steal some inspiration from the massive splendor.

"It's a damn milk commercial," he muttered to himself. "Maybe

I outta drive out to the country and stare at some cows for a while." Zach remembered his last drive in the country. Probably not the sharpest idea.

For Zach, thinking about the accident was quite strange. Such a significant event in his life and yet, the details were nothing more than aborted memories never conceived in his mind. It was sort of like going to a place he had never been to but having a very concrete image of it. He had no recollection of the accident itself and still, it replayed identical in his mind each time he thought about it. It was as if his subconscious had recorded the whole thing on some mental camcorder.

Zach reluctantly snuck a peek at the black-faced Movado that clung to his wrist. After eight already, better phone the wife. He swung his high-back leather chair around to face his cluttered desk and searched for the phone among manila folders and felt tip pens. He exhumed it from a worthless pile of scribble and proceeded to hit speed dial while attempting to assemble some of the mess into smaller, more organized groups of clutter. The voice on the other side answered with a stern "hello" and Zach knew immediately that Katie saw the number on the caller ID.

"Yes Kate, it's me and I know I should have called earlier but …"

Zach also knew that she was more than a little upset as his token attempt to diffuse the situation faltered.

"No, no!" she said sarcastically. "I'm shocked you even called at all."

"Listen, I don't have time for this shit, I just wanted to let you know I'll …"

"So expect you what … around dinner tomorrow, maybe?" Katie cut him off sharply.

"Knock it off Kate, I'll be home sometime tonight, I've just gotta finish up here first."

"Oh, a quickie?" she mumbled just softly enough that Zach wasn't completely sure what she had said.

"What?"

"Never mind," she suddenly realized she wasn't in the mood to argue. "I'm just tired and I think Dove is coming down with something. If you could just be quiet when you come in."

Zach thought better of pushing the issue any further. As it was, an argument didn't much appeal to him either. He still had a lot of work to do and he wanted to get back at it. "Alright, see ya a little later."

"Bye!" And with that, Zach placed the cordless phone down on the desk and swung his chair back around to the window.

"Bitch!" he mumbled as he stood up and began to pace. "Forget it. You've got more important salmon to scalp right now."

He stopped pacing momentarily and placed his forehead against the cold pane of window glass. "Alright Zach, think … think, think, think." He bounced his forehead gently against the window. He wanted to concentrate on the ad campaign; but he couldn't help pondering what he thought Katie might have said about "a quickie."

He figured it wouldn't be too long now before she would confront him about Judith and he knew he had better get his story in order, maybe even rehearse it a few times. He could sense her suspicion with each conversation they'd had of late and the truth was not an option.

He started to pace once again and now, as he stared out into the polluted night, he searched not for inspiration, but rather, for lies. Minutes slid past like seconds as his mind churned feverishly and the soles of his shoes pressed prints into the carpet. He began to notice the fatigue that put a stagger in his step and a sway in his thought.

He sat down in his chair and placed his face into his cupped palms. As he vigorously rubbed his weary eyes, the sound of an opening door injected him with a sudden dose of adrenaline and pulled his mind from his devious ponderings. The creaking noise came from behind him, and when he turned to investigate, the door to his office, previously closed, was wide open.

"Hello! Who's there?" No answer. He walked slowly across the room. *That door had been closed before.* He was sure of it.

Zach got to the open door and popped his head out into the desolate hallway. He scanned its length for another straggler who might be burning the midnight oil. "Hello!" Still, there was no response. There was nobody around. "Must have been a draft or something."

Convinced—well not completely—that all was well, he closed the door and pushed firmly against it. As he walked back toward the window, he threw a quick glance over his shoulder. The door was still closed. When he got back behind his desk, he remained on his feet.

"Good night, city lights," he said as he saluted the skyscrapers outside, dismissing the eerie feeling of not being alone as his tired, overworked mind telling him to close up shop for the evening. He had better be heading back to the suburbs before he got too drowsy. He didn't need to take a nap at the wheel again.

Zach started to turn away from the window when he suddenly felt something on his shoulders. It felt like fingers, or possibly claws. They were jabbing into his shoulder blades with such force that his stance began to collapse like a folding chair beneath him. Whatever it was that had a grip on him did not allow him to fall. He couldn't maneuver to see who … or what … it was that held him upright, so he used the window as a mirror. His solitary reflection mocked him from the darkened glass as the grip on his shoulders tightened. There was nobody behind him and yet; he could feel the tremendous pressure being applied by the unseen, and immensely powerful, intruder.

Suddenly, he felt himself being lifted by the collar, several feet off the carpet. As he dangled in the clutch of his invisible captor, he caught another image in the window in front of him.

This time, however, it was not his reflection superimposed over the city skyline, but rather, that of a man standing naked with his head lowered in a slightly crooked bow. The ethereal figure lifted its drooping head, its gaze finding his in the glass. Zach immediately recognized the reflection in the window. It was Father Kazcmarek.

The old priest grinned unevenly and the madness in his eyes was tangibly sharp and distinct, even against the transparent canvas of glass. He dropped his head back down and charged toward the window, just as he had charged the wall during his suicide. He would have crashed through the glass had he had any actual substance.

Suddenly, Zach felt himself being hurled violently forward. Glass did indeed crash as he began to plummet to the concrete earth forty plus stories below. He screamed and floundered, swinging his arms and legs frantically as he closed in on the corner of 9th Avenue and 45th Street. He remained conscious through the entire decent and when he smacked into the sidewalk a few seconds later, he was still awake. He was still alive.

Zach lay there on his back, staring up at the stars, waiting for death to snatch them instantly from his vision, waiting for an onslaught of pain to justify the horrible thud he heard upon impact. He could not move, not for the moment anyway, and was too scared to try. But there was no pain, not when he hit the ground. Not now. He waited longer still. It never came. How could this be?

A small circle of strangers closed in around him. He gazed up at their anonymous faces as they hovered. There was a petite Asian girl in black fishnet stockings and a fake fur jacket. A thick layer of shoddily applied makeup concealed her complexion but her hiked up mini skirt did little to hide the goods she peddled.

Another prostitute stood to her left. Her—or was it his?—makeup was smeared heavily across masculine features. *It* wore a teased out blonde wig, high heels, and enough eyeliner to make Joan Rivers look like a natural woman. There was a construction worker, a middle-aged yuppie wannabe, and the Jamaican version of the Marlboro Man gathered around him as well.

"Hey mon, you okay?" said the Jamaican as he cupped his hand around a match and lit up a Philly Blunt. So much for Marlboros.

"Yeah, mista," the flannel-clad construction worker added in a native accent as thick as the hookers' Maybelline masks. "That sure was one helluva drop you took there."

Zach sat up in the center of the circle. His eyes brushed over the surrounding spectators, then scanned up the length of the building from which he had just been tossed. Who in the hell … or what in the hell … had thrown him through the window? And how did he not end up all over the sidewalk? This whole ordeal had to be one of those nightmares again. Funny thing was, he could not recall falling asleep.

"We got a little something for your boo boos," the transvestite offered. "Ain't that right China Doll?"

"Sure do baby," the Asian whore agreed as she cracked a bubble of the pink wad she chomped obnoxiously.

Zach got a glimpse of the born again bachelor with the cheap sportcoat and even cheaper cologne. There was something about him that made Zach's stomach quiver and it had nothing to do the pungent odor of too much Old Spice. In fact, they all made him feel uneasy; the construction worker, the Rastafarian cowboy, even the guy in drag.

Zach rose to his feet. He shouldered his way around the Asian whore and began to run. For some reason he felt he had to get away, away from the very people who seemed to come to his aid. Something just wasn't kosher with them.

He urgently navigated his way around, and through, the random clusters of pedestrians that strolled past the caged storefronts and cardboard campsites along 9th Avenue. When he got what he felt was a safe distance away, about thirty feet or so, he slowed to a more leisure pace and glanced back over his shoulder. *Gone!* They were gone, all of them. But how? Did they simply vanish into the night? He knew something wasn't right with them.

Then, at the precise moment he pulled his eyes forward again … *Bang*. Zach slammed right into something. Something solid, unyielding, like a light post or a telephone pole. It stopped him dead in his tracks. Except it wasn't a light post or a telephone pole. It was the yuppie in the cheap suit. Or was it? His face now wore the pale, dry complexion of death and his eyes were unrevealing black stones. He had transformed into some sort of a demon. "Watch it pal! What the fuck is your hurry?"

Zach stared for a moment at the abomination that stood in his path. The terror and confusion that held him in clenched fists squeezed even tighter. "But you ... you were just back ... and ... and your face."

Zach turned to run the other way. *Bang again.* The construction worker didn't budge either. His face too was absent the warm hue of blood. Of life. And his eyes, also solid black.

"Oh shit!" Zach darted from between them. Neither tried to stop him and neither gave chase. He ran for several minutes before ducking into a dark alley between two brick buildings. He slowed to a staggered jog, then into confused exhaustion.

As he continued down the alley, trying to regain a calm rhythm to his breath, he noticed a two-lid dumpster and the large cardboard box that annexed it. One of the dumpster's lids was open, resting against a graffiti-laden wall. This was marked territory. Zach wasn't fluent in gang vernacular but figured it to be a warning of some kind. Now, not only did he have those ... things ... to fear, but the misguided youth of New York, as well. Which was worse?

Zach continued cautiously between the two massive brick walls that formed the alley and soon discovered another warning, this one more direct. The words "BEWARE OF DOG" were scrawled across a paper plate and affixed to the cardboard box with string and masking tape. As he got closer to the dumpster, he could hear a rustling sound coming from within. It frightened him. *Probably just a cat or maybe, one of those giant sewer rats.* But when the second lid burst open, the conviction jumped right out of that idea and Zach nearly jumped out of his skin. Damn sure wasn't a sewer rat.

It was, however, only the homeless man who took up residence in the cardboard chalet. He wore several layers of tattered clothing and a dingy orange cap with frayed yarn sticking out where a tossle once sat. Under his right arm was a collection of discarded newspaper and in his left hand, a partially consumed submarine sandwich he would have to share with the army of maggots that had staked claim to it earlier that evening. "Just grabbin me a midnight snack and a blanket," the old man explained as he took a bite of the sandwich and brushed a few maggots from his knotted gray beard.

Zach began to laugh hysterically. It was the type of uncontrollable outburst that signaled a nervous breakdown. This ordeal was really starting to take its toll on him. "I get it," he bellowed as he pointed to the picture of a chubby bulldog sitting attentively in front of the chrome fridge on the front of the old man's cardboard shelter. "Beware of dog, that's a good one." Even homeless folks can have a sense of humor.

"What a loon!" the old man said to himself as Zach started further down the alley.

Zach reached the junction of the alley and the sidewalk that straddled West 34th. He stepped out onto what was normally a very animated stretch of concrete. On this night, it was completely deserted. Not a pill-peddler or prostitute in sight. The eerie evacuation concerned him. Scared him. Where had everybody gone? This is New York, the city that never sleeps. Tonight, however, it seemed in a coma. No cars … No people … No taxicabs? Only the drawn, yellowish cast of dimmed fluorescent street lamps to show him the way. Only the crackling buzz of a faltering neon sign to challenge the silence.

Maybe it was better that nobody was around. For all Zach knew, anyone could be one of those demon-possessed people, like the construction worker and the yuppie. Maybe there was nobody in sight because there had been some mass exodus back to Hell.

A simple plan formed in his reeling mind. He had to get to his car before they came back. Zach started left on 34th, somewhat bewildered as he scurried across 8th and 7th Avenues without having to watch for the blinking hand on the pedestrian crossing sign or worry about being flattened by a speeding cab.

As he stumbled up Broadway toward the massive, blank screen of the Jumbotron in Times Square, fearful that he might cross paths with … anyone, the Art Deco monster that was the Empire State Building stood tall over his shoulder. He was afraid that whatever those people had transformed into could pop up at any moment. And maybe the next time, they wouldn't let him just run away.

Worse yet, what if they were merely toying with him, like a helpless rodent? Batting him around with playful paws before the inevitable sinking of teeth into raw flesh and brittle bone?

Zach was eleven blocks from the parking garage that sheltered his new 380si and the thought of a rendezvous with that fine piece of German engineering was enough to inject a dose of hurry-up in his step once again. Not surprisingly, it wasn't the heated leather seats or eight speaker sound system that enticed him at the moment.

He crossed the abandoned intersection of 36th and Broadway. On a typical night, the traffic light wasn't the only reason to stop there. But tonight, there was no sex being discounted, no drugs being auctioned. The all-night flea market was closed.

Something, however, did stop Zach. "Ring ... Ring ... Ring."

It was a pay phone on the corner next to Frankie's Pizza, and each ring seemed to utter his name. He didn't want to answer it. He could sense that whoever, or whatever, was on the other side, was calling him, and not just to say hello.

Still, he walked toward it as it continued to ring. He knew it wouldn't stop. Even if he were a hundred miles from a phone, the ringing wouldn't stop and eventually, he would have to answer.

He grabbed the receiver from its cradle, surprised only slightly that it had been severed at the cord, probably by vandals. Hesitantly, he pulled the receiver up to his ear. "Who is it and what the hell do you want from me?"

"Now, Zachary, is that anyway to greet an old friend?"

The voice shot through his brain like pellets from an AK 15. "Judith ... is that you?" He expected the call to be something uncanny in nature, but certainly not from a recently departed ex-mistress.

"How are you my darling?" she inquired in that seductive phone sex voice that once turned him on but now turned his insides.

"Well, let's see," he responded sarcastically, "I'm standing in the middle of Manhattan, which by the way, is totally deserted, having a conversation with a dead ex-lover after falling forty stories and being harassed by demons. I'd say things are pretty much shit right now."

Judith giggled menacingly, "Oh, Zachary, don't worry. Things will be looking up, or should I say down, in no time. Soon, very soon, the two of us will be together again, reunited in the flames of carnal ecstasy."

"No, we will not!" Zach insisted, "I … I'm sorry you died in the accident and I know it was my fault, we shouldn't have even been in the same car … I'm sorry you were killed but …" Zach paused as his own voice began to scream inside of his head, emphasizing once again that he was talking to a dead woman. "Please Judith, just leave me alone."

"But Zach, don't you miss me?"

"Just leave me the fuck alone!" he shouted as he slammed the receiver several times against the rusted lever before heaving it as far as he could down the desolate avenue.

He circled slowly in place, his clenched fists raised above his head and his eyes scanning the thick pillow of smoky pollution that hovered just above the street, "All of you … just leave me alone!"

Zach started to run again. He felt drained and his hard sole shoes barely clung to his feet. However, the thought of getting to his Mercedes without seeing those demons again filled him with energy. He wasn't going to stop for anything, not until he reached his car.

However, as he approached the Jumbotron in Times Square, the giant screen suddenly exhaled a jolting breath of electricity, radiating his ad for Resurrection. He stopped.

From twenty feet away, he watched as his creation flickered out across the square. Even in the midst of near panic, he reveled for a brief moment in self-admiration as the corpse model uttered her single word of dialogue, "Resurrection."

Just then, the word was echoed from behind him. It was spoken much softer this time and yet; the sound of it was unequivocally disturbing, "Resurrection."

The whisper found Zach's ear on sour, exhaled breath. It tickled the back of his neck with a fear that would have dropped him to his knees had it not bronzed him in a cast of disbelief.

Somehow, Judith was standing behind him now. He knew it was her as she pressed her bosom ever so slightly against his back and nestled her chin in the valley between his neck and shoulder. The inconceivability paralyzed him and his heart threw itself violently against his breastbone. It was a reunion with the corpse of an ex-lover, just like in the commercial.

"How did ..."

"Shhh ... don't clutter our precious moment with wasted words," she hushed Zach, then began to gently kiss the back of his neck.

Her lips felt dry and chapped against his skin and, at first, he shrugged in disgust and fear. Then, against deteriorating will, he felt his body begin to surrender to her. Zach was being drawn into her diabolical seduction. His taut muscles relaxed as she sampled the salty glaze that, in spite of the chill in the air, covered his skin. Her fingers eased down the front of his torso, then paused, only for a moment, to undo the snap of his trousers. She forcefully tucked her hand several inches below his waistline. He was already aroused and this brought him to peak. She began to grind her pelvis into his rear and soon he moved in rhythm with her. "Please do not deny me," she pleaded as she nibbled on his earlobe. "I need to taste the mortal sin once more."

Lustful memories coaxed him. Why not just go with it? There was nobody else around. It was just the two of them, alone. The two of them! He and Judith, Judith Sample ... *a dead woman*. This little dose of reality was more intense than any orgasm could ever be and Zach suddenly found himself struggling to escape her seductive grasp. He freed himself and took a few steps forward, then turned to deny her face to face.

What he saw when he looked upon her was not the crimson-haired Aphrodite with porcelain skin and hypnotic eyes he remembered. Rather, it was the spoiled reincarnation of a fallen goddess whose once stunning beauty had been reduced to ash by the inferno from which she had risen.

Her face, like the wax of a partially spent candle, had been melted down and reshaped into something that spared only the slightest tread of its former complexion. Her skin was charred and her mangled hair was tinted with suet and dried blood. She was a rose among weeds in Satan's own garden of fire.

Zach gazed upon her in horror and aversion, retreating as she walked slowly toward him with arms outstretched and her revealing nightie rustling in the brisk breeze. "No, stays back, stay away from me!" he demanded.

"What's the matter Zachary? You don't love me anymore?"

"Love you? I never … just stay away." Zach backpedaled swiftly to regain the dwindling gap between them. Judith continued toward him.

"You are the one that did this to me!" she scowled. "You are the one that diseased my soul! You stole my innocence, and then you stole my life. And what, you reject me now?"

Zach wilted in the scorching fury that shot from Judith's eyes as he felt the barrier between them begin to collapse. "Please Judith, I beg you …"

"You are the reason I will burn eternally in the fires of Hell," she interrupted harshly. "And I am the reason you will soon join me."

"Noooooo," he cried out as he turned to flee but lost the blacktop beneath his feet. He stumbled to the ground as his left arm and hip absorbed the impact. Suddenly, like a child falling from the top bunk, he was jarred … awake.

Zach was back in the black leather chair in his office, hundreds of feet above where he had just been, at least in his head. He regained his equilibrium before scanning the office in search of … well, he wasn't exactly sure. He quickly glanced over at the window. It was completely intact. Not a crack. Had it all been just another one of those horrible dreams? It must have been. And still, he wasn't certain.

He swallowed a few deep breaths, then stood up from the chair. His legs were wobbly beneath him. From fatigue? From fear? Probably a little of both. He was quite disturbed by what he had just experienced, but managed a peek at his Movado. It was late, nearly midnight. Four hours. He had been out for four hours. It seemed more like half an hour. But then again, he had fallen asleep. Hadn't he?

Zach thought about Katie. He decided to head home. Then he thought about Judith. He would be thinking about her for a long time.

As 11:59 gave way to Friday, Zach stepped out into the empty hallway, closing the door of his office behind him. He teetered up to the water fountain on the wall and took a sip from it. The water was cool and refreshing. He cupped a hand under the flowing arch and splashed the water on his face. It was going to be a long drive home.

Zach walked from the fountain rubbing his left elbow. He stopped at the far end of the hallway and pressed one of two illuminated arrows on the wall. It was a long way down to the ground floor. He would definitely be taking the elevator this time.

Chapter Fourteen

Three days later

"A large circle of light appears. Contained within that circle is a picture. It is pressed to the refrigerator door by a Mickey Mouse magnet. Standing at the opposite end of the dark kitchen in his terrycloth pajamas is a young boy. In his right hand is a flashlight, in his left, an ordinary drinking glass."

Larry listened intently to Zach's every word as if some campfire legend was being shared in the glow of crackling pine. He shifted uneasily on the teal leather sofa that oddly complemented the Pepsi machine next to it in the employee lounging suite.

Zach continued. "As the boy tiptoes tentatively across the checkered linoleum tiles, the circle becomes smaller and smaller, closing in around the crayon creation it reveals. A dinosaur, and I don't mean that purple putz with the beer gut. We're talking mean, nasty, with big teeth and sharp claws."

Even though Zach described a child's first grade art project, the image in Larry's head was strictly Jurassic Park. Of course, Zach spoke from the point of view of the little boy in the kitchen; and by the way Larry nervously bit his lower lip, that is exactly the way he heard it.

"This kid is sweating and everything; I mean sis's Mona Lisa has him terrified. But he keeps going. Then, when he gets a few feet away, he puts the flashlight down on the floor, counts to three, and makes a mad dash toward the fridge."

Larry shifted again, as if Zach's words were forging the climax of the next Box Office smash.

"He opens the door and grabs something from inside, then slams it shut and races quickly to the other side of the kitchen. Just then, silence, except for the familiar sound of pouring liquid. When you see the little boy again, he is sitting on the steps, relief on his face and a tall glass of cool CalciYum in his hand. He pulls the glass up to his lips, takes a giant gulp and says, 'Sure hope I get an A on tomorrow's exam'."

For a moment, Larry looked puzzled.

"Don't you get it? If he gets an A on the exam," Zach explained, "then it will go up on the door in place of the picture and the kid won't have to go through all that trouble for a drink again."

Larry shook his head as if the mysteries of the universe had just been unlocked. "Ohhhhh," he said with a wide grin, totally impressed with Zach's idea for the new CalciYum milk substitute commercial. "You are brilliant, a little demented at times, but brilliant."

Zach smiled as he started across the room toward the hallway that led to another hallway that led to another hallway that led to his office.

"And that little kid," Larry continued out loud to himself, "what a trooper, scared shitless and still ..." He chuckled before amplifying his voice to cover the swelling distance between he and Zach, "You could sell a pair of water-skis to a one-legged Amish man."

Zach raised his hand as he rounded the corner into the carpeted labyrinth that was the forty-second floor office of INK Advertising. Two women stood outside of a door labeled "LADIES." The one in her forties with the black roots and black leather skirt, tossed her bleached blonde hair and smiled. The other, a twenty something brunette wearing a much more conservative plaid pantsuit, glared coldly toward Zach's avoiding eyes. "Murdering cheat," she hissed as he slithered by.

Zach turned back toward her but didn't say anything. He really wanted to let her have it. Something along the lines of, "why don't you just shut up you ignorant bitch," would definitely have some therapeutic value, at least for the moment. But Zach simply swallowed the indecent rebuttal like sour CalciYum and proceeded down the hall.

Tiffany Bailey had been friends with Judith Sample ever since the two were brought into the firm together. They went through orientation together and basically shared the paper shuffling duties that always seemed unappreciated and underpaid.

Tiffany blamed Zach for Judith's death. Fact was, several people at the firm did, but Tiffany was the only one who did it to his face. She never much cared for him because she had always believed he would hurt Judith one day.

Her ex-fiancé, Mitchell Cooper, was a cheat too. A truck driver who was on the road for days, sometimes weeks at a clip, he filled up on more than diner grub and diesel fuel at those truck stops along the interstates.

They would have been married three months ago Saturday, a big church wedding with red roses and a four-tiered cake, the whole nine yards, but that lousy bastard had to go and ruin it all. They would have been married had she not found the matchbook in the pocket of his flannel shirt that read, "Next time you're in Pittsburgh, 286-9874, Suzie."

Turned out Suzie was a prostitute, a turnpike whore, the type whose office was the expansive, gravel parking lots of the countless truck stops along the nation's major routes. Lord only knows how many others Mitch had been with. A working girl could always be found at a rest stop full of lonely, horny truckers.

Tiffany didn't blame them for her fiancé's infidelities, however. After all, they were only trying to make a buck, even if she did not condone their career choices. She never blamed Judith for the affair with Zach either. It was always the man's fault; and in this case, the blame most definitely rested on Zach. It was his fault and she let him know it. In the hallway. On the elevator. Anywhere and anytime she could. The stones she could no longer cast at Mitch were aimed directly at Zach. He was, after all, the perfect target.

Zach rounded the corner out of Tiffany's range and the weight of her indignation tumbled off his shoulders. His own festering anger, however, was nearly too cumbersome to bear. With teeth clenched into a rebellious scowl, he turned and headed back toward the rest rooms where the two women chatted, most certainly about him. A few deliberate steps were behind him when he stopped.

He knew there were others at the firm who assigned the onus to him. For the affair. For the tragedy of Judith's untimely death. But only Tiffany Bailey spoke out; and one of these days he was going to let her have it. Eventually, he wouldn't be unable to dismiss her persistent harassment with a turn of the cheek. The only thing that kept him from marching straight back there and letting loose on the bitch right then was the fact that, deep down, he knew that she was absolutely right.

Chapter Fifteen

Katie stared wide-eyed into the white shimmer of evening, held captive in a delicate web of moonlight that gave the season's first snow a subtle sparkle as it fell to earth. The kitchen window through which she gazed captured the portrait of her every breath on its frosty canvas as gray-haired autumn slipped gracefully into retirement.

Just like the newborn winter outside, Katie felt as if she were trapped in a web, a web of deceit woven by the tarantula that crawled up behind her at that very moment.

"Look's like the white stuff's back," Zach commented as he placed his right hand on a shoulder that was even more frigid than the frost on the window.

"Yep," she shrugged and pulled away from him.

"What's the matter?" he questioned in a voice that almost sounded caring.

She intended to tell him that it was nothing, but the voice inside her head told her that this was it. This was the perfect time. That voice inside her head spoke out. "Tell me about her."

"Who?" he responded. He knew exactly who Katie meant.

"Judith," she confirmed in a melancholy tone as she monitored the reaction of his reflection in the window.

"Judith? You mean the woman who ..."

"I mean the woman you had the affair with," Katie became aggressive as a dam of emotion finally broke. "The women you fucked, damn it!" Hostility and resentment accented her words as she battled to control the hurt and anger that flared inside, feelings she had kept to herself for as long as she could. Far too long.

"I what?" Zach retorted in equally firm yet forcefully manufactured anger. "Is that what you think? You think that I had an affair with Judith Sample?"

Katie turned to face Zach. To look him dead in the eyes and read every line of deception that would be revealed within them. "Why were you with her then?"

"With her? I was never …"

Katie cut him off, "With her! With her! Don't give me your bullshit Zach! On the night of the accident! You know damn well what I'm talking about!" She paused to draw a few heavy breaths so she could continue. "Or maybe you've been with her so many times you really don't fucking know which time I'm talking about."

"The accident," Zach agreed readily. "Yeah, of course, I know when you're talking about." Zach had prepared for this very moment a long time ago. He knew eventually it would arrive. The missiles were loaded and he was ready to strike. Just then, he realized that firing bombs wasn't the answer. Of course, he had to deny everything, but a war of words was not the way to attack the situation. "Baby, I love you. You know that. I would never even think of sleeping with another woman."

"Why were you with her Zach?" Katie repeated with staunch resolution.

"Okay, let me explain," he put his hands out in front of him in a calm-down-and-listen-to-me gesture. "She was invited by Raymond Reese, the client I was having dinner with that evening. I don't know, he saw her at the office. He must have found her attractive and I assume she found him, or more likely, his financial situation, appealing because she accepted."

"But it was a party Zach."

"A dinner party Kate, during which we discussed business issues. Men like Raymond Reese throw parties for everything."

She peered deep into his eyes in search of something, anything, that would give him away. *Nothing.* He seemed so sincere; they offered no hint of deception at all. She wanted so desperately to believe him. She loved him immensely and the girls, she couldn't bare to think of the effect this whole thing could have on them.

Dove and Aria, they were the reason Katie could no longer allow her suspicions to fester inside. They were the reason the truth had to come out … tonight. And it started to appear to her as if that was exactly what was happening. She was not, however, completely convinced. "Well, why the hell was she in the car with you?" Katie continued her interrogation.

Zach gained more confidence. His wife seemed to be buying the story. Yes, she was still asking questions, but he could see that her expression, and her suspicion, had softened considerably, "I drove her to the party because Raymond Reese asked me to bring her. Like I said, he thought she was attractive and invited her and she accepted. There was really no sense in us driving up separately. It was sort of a favor I guess, for a very important client."

"So you're telling me that nothing happened between the two of you, ever?" Katie's face slipped into an expression that bordered on relief.

Zach stood there for a moment without speaking. He couldn't help but wonder, as he had done many times since the accident, why the blood test had come up negative. Why they hadn't extracted even a single drop of booze from his veins? The thought, however, was a fleeting one. He didn't have the time to analyze and he certainly didn't have the answers to resolve

"I was just being a friend," Zach answered just before it would appear as if he were stalling. "And the fact that Reese requested her presence made it pretty good business."

"Kissing ass maybe," Katie added.

"Yeah, I guess you could say that. But very innocent, nonetheless."

Zach placed his hand back on Katie's shoulder and this time, she did not pull away. He caressed her cheek with the back of his other hand and gave her a peck on the forehead.

"I never intended to hurt anyone." his voice shuttered with sudden spurts of false remorse. "This whole thing has been ripping me apart inside. I mean the accident and all." Zach took a deep breath as a few manufactured tears trickled down his face. "I've been having these horrible nightmares and I've tried to keep it all bottled up inside but ..."

"Everything's gonna be okay," Katie pulled him into her, wrapping her long arms around his waist. She no longer seemed suspicious of his relationship with Judith and he did a fine job of marketing his counterfeit grief and pulling her further away from that suspicion.

"I took someone's life," he said. "That certainly isn't an easy thing to accept, not an easy thing to deal with. I killed somebody and I'm going to have to live with that for the rest of my life." Zach could sense that Katie had fallen for his little skit and that she believed, or at the very least, accepted, that his relationship with Judith was innocent. She was now more concerned about him, about his mental well-being.

He walked from the window and sat down in the chair that was already pulled out from the table. Katie pulled her chair around the table and settled down a few inches away from him. The emotional scars he exhibited were deep. But in reality, the fact that Judith was dead and he was responsible was little more that an itchy scab in his memory.

"I'm not sure I can continue to work at the firm," he revealed after several reserved moments. "I thought I could go back and deal with everything but now ... I just don't know. People look at me and I know what some of them are thinking."

For the first time in the conversation, Zach stepped out of character. He was, in fact, concerned about his reputation at the office and especially about that bitch Tiffany Bailey. His last line was not a part of the script. And neither was the part about the nightmares.

"You can't worry about everyone else Zach, what those fools think. It was an accident, plain and simple ... an accident." Katie had no idea that Zach had gotten hammered that night. The police found no alcohol in his system and Zach was not about to tell her that they should have.

"Yeah, I know it was, but that still doesn't take away the pain … the pain I caused Judith … her family … my family!" Zach began to sob again and when Katie opened herself to him, he fell into her comforting embrace. "I don't know what I would do, how I could get through this without you."

"You don't have to baby, I'm here for you." Katie gently patted him on the back as she held him close.

Zach had sold her a hefty load. She bought the entire store. He was a master at persuading people to buy other's goods and services … as well as his own lies. He had convinced Katie that the only thing he and Judith had ever shared was a ride; and that was a tremendous weight off his shoulders. Surprisingly though, it didn't make him feel all that much lighter. In fact, there was still something quite cumbersome pushing down on him, something he pondered as he rested his chin on Katie's shoulder. The nightmares. Not everything he told his wife had been a lie.

Chapter Sixteen

One week later

Strobe light caromed off every inch of Euro-Tech decor. Machine generated smoke mingled with cigarette smoke to form a hazy gray cloud that hovered just above the transparent dance floor. Those who moved like specters between the illuminated flickers of fog and color formed a single, oscillating mass.

LeChic was Katie and Zach's favorite nightspot and Zach wasn't quite sure why. They shoe-horned every twenty-something snob with an inflated ego and proper I.D into this giant sardine can on the upper East side, provided of course, you were properly attired. The crowd was smothering enough without the concoction of cologne drenched sweat and stifling smoke that made breathable oxygen that much more scarce a commodity. One had to shell out a twenty spot just for the privilege of surrendering another ten for what amounted to a glass of soda and ice and just enough bottom shelf liquor to make it all seem fun. The music was a belligerent assault on the eardrums and any sustained conversation consisted mostly of "what" and "I can't hear you."

If I have to endure another version of that damn Macherena… Zach's thoughts were impeded by a firm tug on the sleeve of his Nautica shirt. "C'mon hon, let's dance," Katie shouted as Samantha DeAndri stood to her right and coaxed her husband Vince with an enthusiastic wave of the hand.

"What?" Zach moved his face in closer to Katie's.

"I said, let's dance." He processed her request as he slumped in his twisty bar stool and siphoned the last of his Crown and Coke through a partially gnawed stirring straw. Jesus Christ himself couldn't part that sea of bodies. Of course, in Zach's mind, Jesus Christ was nothing more than a mythical entity, like Zeus.

On the other hand, Zach continued to assess the situation. If the girls went out there by themselves, they would most certainly be hit upon by every Rico Suave in the joint.

The verdict was rendered when Zach read Vince's unenthusiastic expression. "Maybe later," he answered. "You girls go ahead." They were, after all, big girls who could take care of themselves.

"Boring!" he could read Katie's lips as she and Sam turned and headed off through the head-bobbing crowd.

It wasn't that Zach didn't want to be there. This was the first time he had been out on the town since the accident and even this overwhelming attack on the senses was good therapy. An entire hour had passed and he hadn't thought once about the accident, or Judith, or the nightmares. He just wasn't in the mood to throw himself into the chaotic mass that seemed frozen around their table at the moment.

"How bout that goal last night?" Vince's dialogue pulled Zach's focus into the confined personal space that hovered over the empty glasses and crumpled cocktail napkins on the table between them. Zach pointed to his ear and shrugged.

"The goal," Vince repeated as he flicked his wrists to simulate a wrist shot.

"Sweeeeet!" Zach replied mocking Vince's hand gestures and nodding.

Vince and Samantha DeAndri were close friends of he and Katie. They met on an Alaskan cruise the two couples took three years ago and developed a pretty solid friendship since. It certainly wasn't uncommon to meet someone from the Big Apple on a vacation, just uncommon to meet someone from New York as genuine and accessible as the DeAndris.

Vince was a hot-stick lineman for the electric company that supplied over four million New Yorkers with power and Sam owned her own beauty salon in Manhattan, the same one that styled Katie's hair so elegantly every three weeks.

"I think I might be able to get my hands on a couple seats for that game against the Penguins next month. Five rows off the glass, smack behind the net," Zach hollered as he tried to suck every last drop of booze off the ice cubes that still remained in his glass.

"Nine rows back, that's awesome!"

"No, I said five rows back," Zach corrected as he held up the thumb and four fingers of his right hand.

"Five," Vince nodded in approval.

Katie and Sam returned to the table when the tempo of the music slowed and couples began to gather for a slow dance. They simply ignored the requests to dance delivered by self-proclaimed studs using pickup lines that hadn't charmed women since junior high.

"Is it later yet?" Katie inquired as she extended a hand to Zach.

Zach hesitated. Then he peeled himself from the stool he had been stuck to for most of the evening and led Katie toward the dance floor, turning his body sideways so he could slice through the crowd more effectively. He needed to move around to get the blood circulating through his legs again; and besides, he simply couldn't resist a Lionel Richie classic.

They stepped onto the floor, which was considerably less congested during slow songs, and began to move in rhythm to the music. Sam and Vince joined them a few seconds later but were far less in sync, as Vince was obviously inflicted with a heavy dose of the white man's disease. Katie wrapped her arms around Zach's shoulders and gave him a peck on the tip of the nose. "Now see, isn't this fun?"

"I was just thinking," Zach started instead of answering her question, "we should take a little vacation, maybe next month. Go down to the condo for a week. Whadda ya think?"

Zach and Katie had invested in a two-bedroom beachfront on Sanibel Island, Florida a few weeks after Zach's first promotion at INK, but had used it only once in that time. Sisters of friends and second cousins had spent a lot more time in it than they had. Zach was still trying to sell off the majority of the prime weeks to help pay for the damn thing. He had known when he signed the papers that he was getting into something he could not afford. He had, however, been climbing rapidly through the ranks at his new company and used his sizable bonus, a lump of cash that dwarfed a lot of yearly salaries, as a down payment. INK certainly was a generous employer and wasn't afraid to throw money at its star executives.

"Do you want to go in December, with Christmas coming and all?"

"I really just need some time away from this place," Zach stated. "I think it would be good for me. We can go early in the month."

"Okay," she agreed somewhat hesitantly," but we'll have to wait till the kids start Christmas break on the 15th."

"I mean just the two of us," Zach clarified as they spun slowly in place and the atmosphere lighting throbbed and spun around them in more subdued patterns.

Just then, Katie's eyes lit up like tiny blue bulbs as a soft smile decorated her face with joyful surprise. Zach hadn't suggested anything like this for what seemed like eons. Just the two of them. That sounded nice. "That would be wonderful, but I'll have to call my sister to see if she'll watch the girls."

Katie knew Pam would take Dove and Aria for the week. She simply adored the girls. Besides, they had watched little Alex when she and Harold went to Las Vegas last May, and that was for ten days. Katie also figured Pam could use the help around the house, getting ready for the holidays and all. Especially since Harold was a lazy ass who definitely had a neck up on the ol' Grinch when it came to anything that involved lights or ornaments.

Katie embraced Zach even tighter as twinkles of silver light imitated stars on the massive ceiling beams above. She closed her eyes and rested her head over his heart as they swayed back and forth. She felt closer to him right now than she had since the honeymoon.

Lately, it seemed as if they had grown apart. She really couldn't explain it. She just felt it deep inside, felt that he had strayed too far out of her life. Little did she know how far he really had strayed.

Chapter Seventeen

Thanksgiving

Passionate discussions of political infidelities and other global misdoings fell off at the mandate of silver tapping crystal. A fleeting giggle severed the silence, but only for a moment. A stern reprimand followed and silence was restored. Lips were now sealed. Heads bowed.

This was the first Thanksgiving dinner hosted by Katie and she had worked tirelessly throughout the morning, and most of the previous evening, to ensure the debut went off without a hitch. It had been ritual for the family to gather at Zach's parents' in Jersey for the late November feast; however, Anne's heart attacked her in January and the doctors advised her not to undertake so rigorous a task as a holiday meal.

Katie and Zach became the obvious choice to inherit what Zach called an honor but Katie considered a monumental responsibility. After a week of bickering between them and a promise of help from Zach, a promise he did not fulfill, Katie reluctantly agreed. Theirs was the largest house of the remaining relatives and Zach's brother, Matthew, lived several hours further away in Altoona, Pennsylvania. Besides, his wife Melanie was more of a helpless child than a Julia Childs when it came to the kitchen.

Twelve people were seated around the elaborate spread that Katie had organized with puzzle-like precision on the oak table barely made sufficient by the insertion of two twelve-inch wooden extensions.

Katie's sister Pamela and her husband Harold sat within easy reach of Ritz cracker stuffing and mashed-potatoes. Seven year old Alex was wedged between them. Matt and Melanie and their nine year old daughter Jennifer were assembled on the opposite side of the table, where a basket of homemade Rye and a large bowl of fruit salad straddled a tray of condiments. Zach's parents Anne and Edward sat next to Dove and Aria while he and Katie were positioned like King and Queen, an equal distance from the succulent golden centerpiece, a fourteen-pound Honeysuckle. Matt's twin boys, Jessie and Michael sat at a smaller table that Katie had set up a few feet away.

Zach sat at the far end of the table, head tilted slightly. He stared into the glass of White Zinfandel on the table in front of him. Like those of the children in the room, Zach's bow was merely a cosmetic, meaningless gesture of conformity. To him, Thanksgiving meant little more than football and food, and spending the day with people he hadn't seen since Easter.

Edward Bell cleared his throat and began to pray. He had always been the one to say Grace at his table and since Zach didn't believe in any of that Catholic nonsense, there was no reason to break tradition.

"Lord, we have many things to be thankful for this year, as we do every year. This bountiful feast of which we are about to partake. The loving family with whom we share it."

Zach sat pokerfaced, following the bubbles in his glass as they shot to the surface. He listened with one ear to the words being spoken, merely out of respect for his father.

"But this year Lord, we have something much more for which we shall be forever grateful, a miracle in its truest form. We almost lost a member of the family this year," Ed's voice trembled and pulled Zach's attention from the wine glass that had preoccupied him. "It is because of this miracle that he sits here with us now, fully recovered from his accident and able to share these precious gifts with those who love him."

Zach glanced at his father, then across the table toward Katie. Sensing his eyes on her, she lifted her head. A tear trickled down her cheek and she smiled. Dove and Aria were seated to her right and she leaned to take a hand of each, clenching their tiny fingers gently in her own. Zach returned a smile as his father's prayer concluded. There was a chorus of "amens" followed by the buzz of tableside prattle which filtered back into the aroma-thickened air.

Katie's eyes were still fixed on Zach's face when his smile suddenly dropped, replaced by an expression she had never seen before. It seemed an expression of utter terror. His eyes now stared past her, or possibly through her; she couldn't tell for sure. His gaze was cold and unwavering.

"Zach, what's wrong? Zach … honey …" Katie swung her arms back and forth in an attempt to summon his attention. He did not flinch.

His focus remained frozen on the wall behind her. His face was tomato-red and he shivered as if the elements that hardened the winter outside had wrapped themselves around his spine. The others seated around the table, now aware of Zach's sudden mental diversion, joined in her concern.

"Son, what's the matter dear? Are you okay?" Anne's delicate motherly tone deflected off him like hail off an umbrella.

Katie looked behind her but saw only the shelf of decorative mason jars and the plaque nailed to the wall that proclaimed, "NO HOME CAN EVER BE COMPLETE WITHOUT THE PATTER OF LITTLE DOG FEET."

Zach, however, saw something completely different. The wall he saw was not the one with the wallpaper that he and Katie had hung last April, with all the pictures of apple bushels and apple cider and apple pies. It wasn't the wall that normally separated the kitchen from the hallway that led to the family room. The wall he saw now was tiled in white and stained with dirt and blood. It was the wall he had seen in his dream, the first dream he had while in the hospital, in the coma.

THE LOBBY

The graffiti was there too, though not all of it was clear as it had been before. He could make out only two images. The pentagram with the Roman numerals he could not decipher and the drawing of the man against tree. The man who was being pulled under the earth by serpent-roots. The man who, in raw, unpolished detail, resembled *him*. Why were these horrible images appearing to him? Following him? What did they mean?

Zach finally broke free of the paralyzing grip that had held him stiff against his chair. He closed his eyes, squeezing them shut as he pulled his hands up to cover them.

"What's wrong with Uncle Z?" little Jennifer questioned as her dad placed a firm hand on his brother's shoulder and shook him gently.

"Hey bro, what's up man?" Matt tried to break through as he shook Zach a little more vigorously. "C'mon Zach, you're starting to scare the kids."

Zach did not respond and Dove's eyes began to swell with tears as she wondered what was happening to her daddy. Everyone at the table wondered exactly the same thing.

Just then, Zach slowly uncovered his face, only partially, as he peeked out over his fingertips with one open eye. The images were still there, still harassing him.

"Noooooo," he screamed with a thunderous roar as he rose up from his chair, sending it toppling to the linoleum floor behind him. He took the unconsumed glass of wine from the table in front of him and flung it across the room, barely avoiding Katie's temple as it crashed against the wall behind her, shattering into tiny pieces that sprayed in every direction.

Matt, who was seated next to Zach, instinctively scrambled from his chair and hurled himself on top of his brother. The two men tumbled to the floor with a thud as an outbreak of what bordered on chaos ensued.

Edward and Harold scurried toward them. Anne clutched her chest as Pam tried to calm her. Children cried and Dove and Aria huddled next Katie who sat in her chair wondering if Zach had been aiming that glass at her. But why would he have done that? Maybe he didn't. Zach had never raised a finger at her before. It couldn't have been her. It was whatever he had seen behind her, or thought he had seen. But what was it? What could have made him flip out like that? Whatever it was, nobody else saw it.

Everyone in the room was either crying, or shouting, or both; and they were all quite stunned by what they had just witnessed.

"What in the hell is the matter with you man?" Matt inquired as he pinned Zach to the floor. Zach was a formidable figure at six-foot-one and two-hundred pounds, but his brother was built like a grizzly bear and had little trouble holding him down.

"Okay, let me up. It's all good now, let me up," Zach requested calmly. "I'm all right, I swear."

Harold helped Matt to his feet before extending a hand to Zach.

"I'm okay, I wasn't throwing at Katie," he assured as he took his brother's hand and pulled himself up. "I wasn't throwing at you sweetheart," he glanced at his stunned wife who still embraced the girls. "I ... I'm sorry."

"Then what the hell were you throwing at?" Katie shouted.

"Alright, now let's everyone just calm down, for the kids," Matt protested as he stood Zach's chair upright, then sat down nonchalantly, trying to lead by example.

Heavy breathing and a few soft whimpers were the last remnants of an episode that seemed to erupt from nowhere.

"What in the world got into you there, Zach?" Pam asked as she peered over at the spot where the glass hit the wall and wasted wine now trickled to the floor. "Why did you throw that glass at Katie?"

"But I didn't throw it at her, I told you." Zach struggled to inject a measure of credibility into his explanation. "It was the wall. There was something on that wall," he pointed with conviction.

"What Zach?" Matt probed, his angry voice tempered with concern. "What about the wall?"

Zach's conviction quickly faded. If he told them what he had really seen, they would certainly find it preposterous. Hell, they would think he was crazy, the way he was starting to think of himself. Zach glanced back over at the wall. The images were gone. It was just the damn kitchen wall. It had probably always been just the kitchen wall? Maybe he was crazy.

"What's up with the wall?" Matt repeated.

Zach took one last peek past Katie, "I … I don't know exactly."

* * *

10:48 P.M.

A swallow of nervous anticipation. The shuffling of magazine pages. The faithful ticking of the silver alarm clock on the night stand. Every sound seemed amplified against the soft surroundings of the bedroom.

Katie and Zach sat up in bed. Pillows cushioned their backs as they leaned against the solid oak headboard they had purchased from a small Amish furniture store near Lancaster. It was one of those handcrafted pieces with clamshells carved into the wood that costs three times as much as the mattress, frame, and box springs put together.

"I've been seeing things lately, really freaky things," Zach revealed when silence could no longer contain the weight of words he had been arranging in his mind for the past fifteen minutes.

"Huh?" Katie responded, her attention committed to an advice column somewhere between the cover of January's edition of one of those women's magazines that men leaf through when their wives aren't around.

"I said I've been seeing things, nightmares I guess, only I'm not sleeping," Zach paused. "Like earlier at dinner."

Katie's focus was immediately pulled from the article that she had been dissecting under the dim light of the lamp on the night stand.

"Well, they started out as nightmares but lately …" Zach swallowed nervously, then continued, "I wasn't totally honest with everyone when I said I had a vision of the car crash … you know, when

I flipped out at the table." After a measure of calm had been restored to their Thanksgiving celebration, Zach had convinced the family that he was reliving the accident in his mind and that the doctors told him it was a totally normal occurrence after such a traumatic experience.

Katie placed the magazine on her lap and Zach closed the copy of Men's Health he had been staring through while agonizing over exactly when and how to introduce the subject of demonic sightings to his reasonably well-grounded wife of nine years. Now that he had her undivided attention, he wanted desperately to take back what he had just said, to simply rewind the last forty seconds and forget all about them.

"Alright, so then what was going on at dinner?"

Too Late.

"I don't want you to think I'm crazy." Funny, that's exactly the impression he was starting to have of himself. "I don't know if the accident did something to my brain, the coma maybe, but I've been seeing … things … ghosts."

"Ghosts!" Katie laughed skittishly, hoping that this was all just a big joke.

"Well, not exactly ghosts. They're more like … demons. I don't know, maybe I am nuts, but I've been seeing this stuff and it's really starting to scare the shit out of me."

He was serious, Katie surmised, as the expression on her husband's face surrendered no hint of letting her off the hook. Dead serious.

"Demons? In this house?" she questioned uneasily.

"Well, sort of, yes. In the house, at work, on the street."

"And what do these … these demons look like?" When Katie said the word "demons" the whole thing just sounded so irrational.

How was he going to describe his visions without coming off like some kind of a flake? He didn't want to sound like one of the girls after they cried out from their room across the hall or timidly stood at the side of the bed begging to spend the rest of the night with mommy and daddy. He wasn't sure if his tales would sound more like Dove's closet monsters, the ones with the shovel-shaped foreheads, or the scary, spider-armed clown under Aria's bed. He only knew they would sound considerably more absurd coming from someone who should have outgrown his Bogeyman phobia two decades ago. "It's not like little red guys running around with horns sticking out of their heads or anything," Zach started to explain after a long pause of deliberation. "In fact, today it was only pictures on the wall.

"Pictures?" Now Katie was really confused.

"Drawings, more like drawings. Really sick graffiti. A pentagram surrounded on three sides by numbers, Roman numerals actually, IX, I, III. And then there's the man leaning against a tree. Except the tree is alive; it's pulling the man into the ground. Today wasn't the first time I saw these drawings either."

"And the demons, did they draw these pictures?" Katie sounded smug and sarcastic even though it was really quite unintentional.

She did not doubt that Zach had seen, or at least, thought he had seen these things he described with such emotion, not when she remembered how he had acted at dinner earlier that evening. The way he hurled the glass at the wall. And the terror in his in his eyes.

Zach smirked, "I shouldn't have said anything. I knew it would sound absolutely ridiculous."

"No, Zach," Katie quickly intervened, "I believe you, I do. At least that you think you saw those things."

Zach leaned to his right and placed his reading glasses and the magazine next to the alarm clock on his nightstand. He chugged the water from a glass on the stand before placing it over the face of the masculine bicycle-riding stud on the magazine cover. He rubbed his eyes for no particular reason, then fell back against his pillow again. *I believe you. Don't fucking patronize me, you bitch.* What's next? One of those little speeches you give to the girls about your god sending each of us an angel to protect us when we sleep?

"I think maybe I'll give that Dr. what's-her-name a call, the one your sister was telling us about." Zach decided against any hostile rebuttal to what he read as obvious patronization. Besides, how could he blame his wife if she didn't believe him? Hell, he had trouble believing himself.

"Simmons, Cheryl Simmons, I think," Katie recollected.

Earlier that evening, Pam had given Zach a business card with the name and number of Dr. Cheryl Simmons, the person she credits with helping her to "salvage sanity and soul." Dr. Simmons was the psychiatrist who treated her and Harold after the miscarriage of what would have been their second child. Pam was so distraught, so disillusioned, she nearly took her own life three weeks after unforeseen complications took the life of the unborn fetus inside of her.

It was a Tuesday afternoon and Harold had been back to work for almost a week. If little Alex, who was thirteen months old at the time, hadn't woke up crying in his crib, Pam would have pulled the trigger on her husband's twelve gauge and all of the anguish, all of the suffering, would have splattered along with her tonsils on the living room wall behind her. And if it hadn't been for Dr. Simmons, Pam swears it could have come down to swallowing that barrel again, and probably a mouthful of six shot.

She too had suffered from nightmares, visions. They were a result of what Dr. Simmons diagnosed as Posttraumatic Stress Disorder; and they harassed her every night for months. Even now, eight years later, disturbing images of the unborn child periodically surfaced in the upheaval of a peaceful night's rest. *A faceless child, without form or definition, without age or gender. But always crying, always condemning.* Dr. Simmons taught her how to deal with the pain and cope with the nightmares. Pam still called her on occasion, "just to keep up on my lucidity."

"I think I just need this vacation. That's exactly what the good doctor herself would probably order," Zach inferred as he tried to sink his back deep into his pillow and his mind even deeper into the Gulf of Mexico. "If that doesn't do the trick, I'm gonna set something up with that Sampson as soon as we get back from Florida."

"Simmons dear," Katie closed the magazine that had been draped over her lap and transferred it to the nightstand on her side of the bed. She fluffed her pillow and set it down flat on the mattress. She flicked off the lamp and the details of the room tucked themselves away into the folds of darkness that settled like a blanket over them. "Whatever you think is best baby," Katie laid down, nuzzling her face against Zach's hip. "Just remember, I'm here for you."

Zach remained upright against the headboard. He stared into the vacant darkness that took form like a body cast around him. "I hope this vacation is all I need to get back on track." He paused, "That Sanibel sunset always seems to do wonders for my psyche."

Chapter Eighteen

Vacation, day one, early afternoon

Pelican Cove Condominiums flanked a stretch of pristine private sand referred to by Katie and Zach as Solarcane Beach. There was good reason for the nickname.

It happened on their first visit to Sanibel Island, a quiet Gulf resort crowned by Captiva Island and the upscale playground of South Seas Plantation and separated from Ft. Meyers by a toll bridge constructed to discourage so called "riff raff" from souring the flavor of this upper class paradise. Day one of a four-day weekend escape and Zach, using typical macho rationale, had decided that, because it was February—it didn't matter that it was eighty-five degrees—sunscreen was a nuisance with which he need not bother. He had, more or less, challenged the scorching Florida sun to a game of Chicken, and in the process, ended up fried. He was confined to the forgiving shade of the condo for the remainder of the trip, and had they not purchased that very same condo the following month, Zach would probably still be sleeping on the floor with Mojo.

Now, hundreds of high-tides and spectacular sunsets later, another Sanibel vacation was in jeopardy even before the first umbrella was opened in a tall frosted glass of partially frozen coconut flavored liquor.

Zach knew that Katie would be out of the bathroom in a matter of seconds and that he had better find an adequate hiding place before she was. He crumpled a pair of pink lace panties in his right hand, the ones he had just discovered in the second drawer of the wicker chest across from the bed. Judith had obviously forgotten to pack them when she and Zach were down in late July during a supposed advertising convention in Scotsdale, Arizona. His eyes desperately scanned the room. His heart and his mind darted like whipped thoroughbreds at the track. Then, the bathroom light went out.

"Shit!" Even though Mexico was nearly five hundred miles southwest of where he stood, Zach felt like a piñata swinging helplessly in an open air plaza; and if Katie caught him with another woman's lingerie, she would start to whack him with that big old stick of suspicion and he would have to spill a whole lot of sweet bullshit before she stopped.

With the distinct motion of a professional bowler—after a couple six packs of malt liquor—he flung the crumpled ball of evidence under the bed, just as Katie rounded the corner.

"What in the world are you doing?" she questioned.

"Damn mosquitoes," he replied without hesitation.

"Well c'mon, let's hit the beach. We can unpack the rest later." Katie sported a pair of Raybans and a revealing silver two-piece and looked more Baywatch than she had since before the girls were born.

Whew! That was close. Zach slung a New York Giants towel around his neck and grabbed the bottle of Coppertone spf 38 from his suitcase. "Don't forget this," he held the lotion bottle out in front of him. He would have to ensure proper disposal of the evidence later.

Katie chuckled, "I've got some in my beach bag, lobster boy."

"Very funny!"

As they stepped from the air-conditioned comfort of the condo into the unquenchable mid-afternoon sun, Zach wondered how he could have been so careless when double and triple checking every corner of the condo prior to departing from his steamy weekend getaway with Judith.

"I could have sworn I checked every drawer," he muttered to himself.

He knew the panties were Judith's, not only because nobody

had used the place since he and Judith were there, but because he was the one who bought them for her, at Frederick's of Hollywood he recalled. And because he remembered how much fun he had peeling them off of her.

* * *

8:25 P.M.

A stuffed alligator wore a straw hat and plastic bib. A cross-eyed toucan held a welcome sign in its paper mâché beak. An autographed snap shot of Jimmy Buffet strumming his guitar in a wooden rowboat under the shade of Red Mangrove trees hung crocked in a seashell frame. And the music of Danny Morgan, the self proclaimed Jimmy Buffet of the islands, spilled out into an already festive atmosphere that danced around their table in true Parrot-Head style.

The Mucky Duck was Zach's favorite restaurant on the islands, maybe on the entire planet. The Big Apple certainly had its fair share of celebrated dining establishments, but none was more authentic in its charm and personality—tacky but genuine—than this humble little thatched hut nestled on a stretch of beach renowned for its spectacular sunsets.

People would converge on the sand right across the way, a hundred or more during the winter tourist season, to watch the sun drop behind the endless rippled horizon of the Gulf. It wasn't hard to imagine someone behind the earth, pulling gently on the string of an enormous yellow balloon until it disappeared below the edge of the sea.

A bell rang out, calling attention to a table wedged into the corner beneath a large white inner tube labeled "U.S.S MINNOW." Heads shifted and conversations hushed. It was that charismatic fellow who greeted everyone at the door, the one with a native tan that bronzed him from balding head to sandaled toe. Where else could you find a restaurant owner shaking the hand of an arriving patron with a joy buzzer or fooling an unsuspecting diner with a fake beer mug? "Folks, can I please have everyone's attention for a moment?" the jovial gentleman requested in a deep Sicilian accent. "We have newlyweds dining with us this evening."

The bashful young couple, a heavy set man in his mid-twenties and the brunette Zach considered much too beautiful for a fat slob like him, kissed over their Surf n Turf for two as the full house applauded and tapped their glasses with silverware. This was the type of woman he would go for if he weren't married ... to someone who was in the same room at the time.

As Katie peered over at the honeymooners, she remembered how she and Zach had once shared that intense affection. The newness that filled each encounter with mysterious anticipation. The way it felt almost orgasmic just holding hands. And the flawless sparkle in his eyes every time he looked upon her. That is what Katie saw in the eyes of the young lovers who were celebrating a promise of eternal devotion. That is what she hoped she would see when she gazed back across the table. But Zach's eyes were empty. It was a vacancy only she could notice.

He flashed an elastic smile toward her before dropping his face back down behind the menu he held out in front of him like a copy of the Times. Why had that sparkle faded? It had been so glorious on their wedding day, so radiant all those times they spent together in the oak groves at U.V.

"I love you," she mumbled.

"I think I'm gonna have the fillet." Not exactly the response she was seeking.

She reached across the table and pulled on the menu behind which Zach seemed to be hiding. "I said I love you."

"Oh, I love you too sweetheart," he replied with all the sincerity of a mini-mart clerk working on Christmas Day.

"Do you really?"

"Of course babe. Now you better decide what you want because the waiter will be back shortly."

Katie opened her menu and lifted it up to eye level. She glanced back over at the newlywed couple who still seemed enthralled. "Isn't it sweet, so in love, like nothing else in the world could possibly matter."

"Yeah," Zach said as he placed his menu on the table and scanned the assorted oddities that gave the place its tacky charm. "It seems that way when you can still count the number of days you've been married on the same hand that's holding your fork. They'll get over it."

Get over it? Katie had to consciously press her lips together to throttle the unpleasant response that nearly pushed past them and would have almost certainly totaled the remainder of the evening. She wanted to ask him what in the hell he meant by "get over it." What, the way he had gotten over her? It was both *what* he said and *the way he said it* that started her wondering about Judith Sample again. So matter-of-factly. Get over it. How many other women had he gotten over? And under? And behind?

Suddenly, her suspicions about Zach's relationship with Judith, the ones that had evaporated when he suggested this vacation for just the two of them, swelled like high tide.

"Are you folks ready to order?" a twenty-something waiter with sun-dyed skin stood tableside, his lifeguard's physique stretching the fabric of a green Polo style shirt with the words "Mucky Duck" stitched across the pocket.

Somewhere near the tip of Katie's tongue, the words "Are you sure you haven't been sleeping around?" translated as, "I'll have the broiled swordfish with lemon spritz." She requested sour cream on her baked potato and handed her menu to the server.

As she sipped from the glass of spiced rum and pineapple juice that had just been placed in front of her, she felt a sense of curious relief that the waiter had come to take their orders when he did. Maybe it was better she didn't say anything about Judith Sample right now. They were, after all, on vacation. Besides, she was probably just overreacting. She peered across the table at Zach as he pointed to his menu and discussed various shades of pink with the waiter. She couldn't help but wonder.

Chapter Nineteen

The final night in paradise

On this night, the sea was angry. The normally placid surf of the gulf clobbered the beach with wave after unrelenting wave of discontent. There was no storm out beyond the horizon, no whipping winds to stir the sea so restless in its vast cauldron. So why did it seem to boil with such intensity? Such rage? Maybe there was strife within the ocean's tyranny, a challenge to the throne of Poseidon. Zach sensed that it was something else entirely.

For Katie, the ocean's song was the lullaby that had eased her gently into a tranquil slumber some half an hour earlier. For Zach, however, each foamy tumble battered away the sleep he could not summon by closing his eyes. The sea raged in raw discord and, as he listened closely, its salty voice seemed to call his name, "Zachary!"

He rolled over on the mattress that had furnished him with six restful nights. On this, the seventh and final night of their stay, however, the comfort of quality bedding did little more than taunt his weary bones.

Zach now faced away from Katie and toward the moonlit sea. As he struggled against the nervous grumblings he couldn't quite put reason to, he noticed a sudden flash of light through the sliding glass doors that led out onto the screened in patio overlooking the condo's private beach. There was another flash, then another.

At first they were faint, distant jabs of yellowish white, many miles out to sea it seemed. But with each flicker, they grew more intense, more powerful, until the entire room throbbed like a disco tech.

Zach tried to ignore it, to dismiss it a passing cruise-liner or shrimping boat. It was not. Somehow he knew it. He could feel it. Besides, the beams were much too bright now. They seemed to be searching for something and he was certain they had found it. Found him.

"Zachary ... Zachary!"

Zach was not asleep. The unease he felt would not afford him that luxury. If this was another of those bizarre episodes—and it appeared to be just that—an unpleasant dream couldn't possibly be the culprit.

He tried to close his eyes, but curiosity would pry them open again. He pulled the covers up over his head and buried his face in the pillow. But even that could not deflect the strobes of light that were being injected into the room and into his soul. He did everything he could to fight the urge to give in and investigate. He was being seduced by something much stronger than himself, something he knew was evil. He finally surrendered to its calling. He had no choice.

"Zachary," the sea beckoned over and over.

Zach emerged hesitantly from beneath the covers and swung his feet over the side of the bed. He sat for a moment at the edge of the mattress and then used both arms to push himself upright. His knees felt weak but did not give. He stood for a moment, trying to resist the light, but it seemed to draw upon the fear that was building inside him and soon he was walking toward the sliding glass door. Katie remained asleep, undisturbed by her husband and the flashes of light that provoked him.

Naked down to the low rise briefs that he wore to bed, Zach grabbed his robe from the back of the chair closest to the door and wrapped himself in it, tying the silk belt snug to his waist. For a brief moment, it gave him a sense of security. It was a false sense.

He softly slid the glass doors open and stepped barefoot onto the concrete patio. He stood there, using his hand like a visor to shield his eyes from the searing light flashes that branded a rhythmic pattern into the night. He could hear a distant hum above the water. The sound moved closer, rising above the chaotic roll of the sea.

Suddenly, a swarm of ... something ... broke through the hovering darkness in a single gray quilt sewn across the horizon. *Cicadas?* Like kamikaze pilots, they slammed themselves into the mesh mosquito screen that enclosed the patio; and as they pelted it with their tiny bodies, they dropped two stories to the salty grass below. Zach realized that they were indeed cicadas and that this was indeed another episode. He also realized that he was trapped helplessly within its grip, forced along by the hand of some unseen evil that played with his body and his mind. Had he become a pawn in Satan's own chess match?

Zach was bronzed in fear as he witnessed what appeared to be a mass suicide of cicadas. Or were they trying to get at him? Whatever the case, the onslaught ceased a few moments later. The light, however, did not. And neither did the voices that called to him in the turbulent tide, "Zachary!"

Zach descended the spiral staircase that led to a glass enclosed area where he and Katie stored their rental bikes. It too had a sliding door and he hesitated only briefly before he approached it. As he unlatched the lock and began to slide the door open, something crashed into it as well. Something much larger than an insect. It hit with such a thud, in fact, that Zach jumped backwards. He lost his balance as he stumbled into the bicycles behind him and nearly dropped on top of them. "What the fuck was that?" he gasped as he caught himself on the metal railing of the staircase. He held his right hand up to his chest. His heart, which had already been anxious in its rhythm, now pumped his coursing blood in quick, violent spurts.

He walked cautiously back toward the partially opened door. There was a jutting blossom of cracks in the glass and a single ruffled feather held to it by a slimy mixture of blood and guts. At the base of the door, lying dead among the fallen cicadas, many of which had not survived their own impact, was a bird. Zach was able to identify it as an Osprey because he and Katie had taken an island wildlife tour earlier that week.

This one, however, was somewhat more difficult to recognize than those they had admired from the relative comfort of an open-air tour bus. It was mangled and twisted and covered with those cicadas that were still alive and already devouring the fresh carcass. He did not want to step outside and onto the breathing mound of ravenous insects, but the flashing light and the sea called to him. He was without options. Without control.

With one long stride, he attempted to hurtle himself over the gruesome banquet. He could not avoid all the insects; there were simply too many, and cicadas crackled under his bare feet as he made his way across the moist grass to a set of four wooden steps. He took each step cautiously, grasping a railing of glorified two-by-fours with his right hand in case his trembling legs failed him. When he got to the top he turned toward the light that, with each flicker, encased him in a brilliant yellow cast. Just as it fell off his illuminated frame and speckled sight returned, another flash struck him.

Zach stood at the beginning of a wooden boardwalk that stretched from the entrance of the swimming pool to the beach some thirty yards straight ahead. The sea continued its assault on the sandy shore, hurling six-foot waves that crested silver in the brilliant shimmer of the full moon. The dazzling white circle hung like a massive pendant against the dark breastbone of the sky and illuminated the way as Zach paced the length of the boardwalk. Each weathered plank he stepped upon creaked in soft protest whispered against the bellowing sea. He didn't know where he was walking to, or why, only that some unseen force guided him there.

He came to the end of the boardwalk and walked down the wooden ramp that sloped onto the sand. The flickering beam, the one that he had hoped was only a boat, disappeared. He scanned the horizon but the light was gone.

"Zachary," the voices of the sea, however, still called to him, urging him toward the water's edge. As dry, coarse sand absorbed each step, he trampled clusters of shells that gathered on the shore. Residencies outgrown and disregarded by the tide, the shells sliced into his tender feet like tiny Ginsu knives. With each excruciating step, his knees buckled and he bellowed out in agony.

Still, he proceeded toward his unknown destination, pressing a trail of bloody footprints into the beige sand behind him. The initial step onto sea-soaked sand was nearly unbearable; and when the first drift of salty water swelled around his ankle, he could walk no farther.

This definitely wasn't a dream. The pain was much too genuine. Zach gazed down at the wounded feet he lifted in inspection. There were lacerations carved into them and he grimaced as another rush of salty water washed over them. When the water receded, the blood was gone; but it quickly reappeared before the next dying wave cleansed the wounds again. Even though sparks of pain shot up the entire length of his legs, he did not try to stop or retreat. He knew that there was no use.

Why had he been summoned to the edge of the ocean? He looked. He listened. And he smelled. A pungent odor suddenly emerged from the bowels of the sea, the scent of rotting fish. It made him gag. What in the hell was that smell? Zach pulled his hands up to cover his face. He glanced back down to the sand. The answer had washed up with the rushing tide and collected around him. It was fish, dead fish, and not just one or two, but hundreds, maybe thousands. Zach looked left, then right. The entire beach, as far as he could see, was littered with dead fish. "What is going on here?" he shouted.

There was no response. In fact, now there was silence. His eyes peered forward. The waves had ceased and an eerie calm prevailed … for the moment. The moment was brief, just long enough for Zach to throw another glance toward his bloody feet. He could not look the pain away though it was less than before. He picked his head back up. The water was now bubbling and steam rose from its rippling surface like a resurrecting spirit. The air, already sticky and humid, began to gel and close in on him. He broke into a sweat, beads at first, and then pools that soaked him thoroughly. The heat intensified. His skin started to burn. It felt as if he were trapped in a vegetable steamer. A hundred and fifty degrees, at least. *Rising ... one seventy-five ... two hundred.* Zach gasped for oxygen and his skin began to shrivel.

The Gulf of Mexico was boiling. And the moon, the moon was engulfed in flames. The massive ball of fire was cooking the sea ... and Zach. He tried to run but he couldn't. It was as if the sand was now concrete and his feet had sunk down into it, ankle deep. He tried to free them but they would not budge. He turned away from the moon, using his arms to shield his eyes from its scorching glare. Then, all at once, the glare was gone ... and the heat.

Zach lowered his arms. He gazed out over the water. The moon had disappeared. Something had eclipsed the colossal planet of fire ... and that something was rumbling toward him. He squinted to get a better view. It was a giant tsunami, maybe a hundred feet high, and rolling rapidly to shore. As it tumbled closer, Zach could see that it was no ordinary tidal wave. He had never witnessed a real one before, but he was certain that what he saw was not typical.

"Zachary, were waiting for you to join us," the wave, or something within the wave, spoke to him, "waiting to feast upon the spoils of your mortality." The voices grew louder. They were the same voices that had lured him from his pillow, only now they were much sharper, much more defined. There was moaning too, a serenade of suffering.

As the wave coiled a few yards away, ready to strike with the precision of a serpent, Zach could make out apparitions within its salty detail. Human souls tossing and spilling over into themselves. Their naked forms were abstract, elongated, adopting the shape of their watery domain. These were condemned spirits, slaves of eternal damnation, held in spiraling captivity. Soon, if he could not free his feet from the sand, Zach would join them.

His struggle, however, was fruitless and panic gave way to surrender. Certain death was seconds away. He dropped to the sand and curled his head between his knees, clasping his hands on the back of his neck. Muscles stiffened. Eyes closed. He knew the wave would shatter him.

The massive tube was directly above him now and he released a muffled shriek, waiting for death to collapse around him. Waiting for silence. Then, all at once ... "Excuse me sir."

Zach felt a hand on his shoulder. "Excuse me, are you okay mister? Mister? *A female voice.* Zach slowly pulled his head from between his knees and gazed upward. A young woman in a flowered sun dress stood hunched over beside him. Her husband lingered a few steps behind, throwing a concerned glance toward her.

Zach looked around, his mind still poised against the death that had been inevitable only seconds before. The sea was calm and the moon was white. The sand that bonded him to the beach had been washed away from his ankles and the lacerations in his feet were gone too.

"What's wrong?" the twenty-something man probed as he grabbed his wife's arm and pulled her gently back to him. He wore swim trunks and a flowered button-down shirt that looked like something straight out of Don Ho's closet. Only the bottom two buttons were fastened and the garment drooped off his slender shoulders.

Zach broke into a fit of hysterical laughter as he uttered a single word, "insane."

The couple, who had been strolling hand in hand along the beach, navigated cautiously around him. Now concerned with their own well-being, they moved swiftly across the sand, turning to look back only when the gained sufficient distance. What they saw was a quivering heap that the receding tide could not pry away from the shore and carry out into the depths. What they saw frightened them and they quickly scurried farther down the beach, not stopping again to look back.

Zach's laughter halted. He stood up. The wobble just below his kneecaps threatened to drop him right back down to the sand. He steadied himself before it did.

Then, like a zombie, he trudged back toward the boardwalk that led to the condo, never looking anywhere but straight ahead. He barely noticed that there were no longer bloody footprints in the sand leading to the beach, not even where the water couldn't possibly have erased them. It was as if he had never walked on the beach at all. He paid no mind to that little oddity because his mind was drained of all but one solitary thought. *I must be going mad.*

Chapter Twenty

Hope. Joy. Inner peace. The inspiring motif in Cheryl Simmons' office conveyed what many who sat among it were there to discover, or rediscover. It wasn't as if the troubled could simply extract the medicine for their aching souls from the painting of an orange-winged Monarch napping on a daisy in a sun-washed meadow, but at least the walls around them didn't accentuate the gloom they harbored inside of them.

As Zach slouched in the beige chair of softened leather next to a bouquet of mixed wildflowers in a crystal heart vase, the cheery feel of his surroundings did little to brighten the murky shade of his thoughts.

He was here, as others before him, willing to spill his insides, to volunteer the darkest, most personal details of a life that seemed to be careening out of this reality and into some obscure, horrible place he found himself in from time to time. It was as if he no longer had jurisdiction over his own mind, his own thoughts. Now, it seemed, someone ... or something ... from that loathsome place possessed his brain and manipulated his thoughts, not only when he slept, but whenever it wanted.

To discuss the whole thing with a complete stranger was definitely not something Zach felt comfortable doing, but it seemed a minuscule ransom to offer whatever it was that held hostage his fragile sanity.

There was that one hundred-dollar an hour toll as well. But Dr.

Simmons was a fine psychiatrist, one of the elite in her field, and if she could somehow help him to escape from, or at least, cope with, whatever the hell it was that had pushed him here in the first place, it would all be worth it.

Answers. Reason. A voice of conviction. A voice other than his own. Someone to make sense of it all and to make it all go away. Cheryl Simmons represented what Zach was beginning to accept as his only hope. She definitely offered more than the pot of gold at the end of the ceramic rainbow that sat on the glass coffee table in front of him.

"Hello, Mr. Bell, sorry to keep you waiting, I'm Dr. Simmons."

Zach gazed up—hopefully not to obvious in lust—at a tall slender woman in her early forties, ten years of which had been stripped away by recent cosmetic adjustments. Her conservative attire left much to the imagination but the white blouse she wore under her peach vest did allow a peek of cleavage, surgically adorned no less, where the material yawned between the second and third buttons.

"Nice office!" Zach commented as he stood to shake the manicured hand that the doctor extended out in front of her. He was careful not to reveal the attention he paid those buttons.

"Please sit Zach. May I call you Zach?"

"Of course. And you're Cheryl, correct?" Zach gently took her hand for a moment that lingered a bit beyond casual, then slumped back down into the chair, regaining the warmth of his own body from its swelling cushions.

"Actually, I prefer Doctor Simmons," she responded matter-of-factly before giggling. "Just a little ice-breaking humor. Cheryl is fine."

Zach smiled. He suddenly felt at ease, much more so than he had anticipated anyway. He always seemed to feel comfortable around attractive woman; and Dr. Simmons was definitely aging as delicately, and tentatively, as modern cosmetic procedure would permit.

"Would you care for a drink? I have a bottle of Lagavulin."

"Scotch?" he replied, totally surprised that this psychiatrist was offering booze to her patient.

"I like my clients to be relaxed." Dr. Simmons never used the word patient, at least not in the presence of one. She felt it sounded too judgmental and would put them immediately on the defensive. "The relationship I strive to achieve with them is informal, sort of like a best friend with whom one would confide anything. I find that type of relationship to be much more conducive to progress."

She walked across the room and secured a bottle from a small cabinet behind a contemporary wrought-iron table she employed as a desk; she didn't have one of those cherry-wood Goliaths with an abacus and engraved nameplate. In fact, none of the furniture in the office would have seemed out of place in a living room designed directly from the pages of an Ikea catalog.

"In that case, make it a double, no ice." Zach shifted in his seat as the doctor pulled two glasses from the cabinet and placed them on the table. She filled each halfway to the rim before setting the bottle down.

"So, I understand you were involved in a pretty serious automobile accident," she began as she strode back toward him with the glasses of scotch in her hands. She handed him one before settling into the chair directly across from him.

"Thank you," Zach sampled the drink, puckering as the alcohol burned the back of his throat and twisted his sinuses. "Yes, back in September."

"Did you want water in that?"

"Oh no, this is fine … perfect," he took another sip, trying desperately not to look like a grade-schooler taking his first swig of Mad Dog in the football field after classes.

Dr. Simmons slammed her drink without so much as a tweak of facial resistance and placed the empty glass on the table between her and Zach. "And you were in a coma?"

"Yes, but only for eighteen hours," he answered as he stared, quite impressed, at the empty glass the doctor had just made light work of.

"You were very fortunate," Dr. Simmons surmised.

Zach nodded half convinced. He certainly didn't feel fortunate. In fact, he felt like shit. He wasn't getting much rest and there was always the threat of a relapse.

Without warning, he could suddenly be yanked back into the Twilight Zone, pulled through the cracks of a wall that divided reality and the confused terror of whatever it was on the other side. It was a wall that seemed to be crumbling all around him.

Just then, the room went dark. The circle of light that had been cast upon the ceiling by the sleek halogen lamp across the room devoured itself with a tapered buzz. For a long moment, every object in Dr. Simmons' office translated to an anonymous gray shape, every detail absorbed into a shroud of obscurity. Zach could feel the panic begin to swell as he sat plastered in fear, waiting for ... something.

A few seconds later, seconds that spent like hours in Zach's mangled perception, light returned, placing him mercifully back into the reality he had left only moments before. He scanned the room for verification before he planted his sight on Dr. Simmons. She was still seated across the table from him.

"Damned wiring in this place," she groaned. "That happens every time someone in the building uses a copy machine or a paper shredder. I don't know how many times I've told Carl about that."

Zach mustered relief in a deep, calculated breath and, as he exhaled, the tension peeled away like dead skin. He downed the last several mouthfuls of caramel liquid in one harsh gulp, trying to sand the sharp edge off his frazzled nerves. "With all the shit that's been going on in my life lately, I can't say I feel all that fortunate."

"Going on? You're referring to the nightmares?"

Zach was visibly shaken now. *Nightmares?* Lady, a nightmare would be holiday time compared to what's been going on in my life. He placed the empty glass on the table in front of him. His hand trembled and he pulled it quickly to the armrest at his side.

"That's the thing. I'm not so sure that they are nightmares."

Zach buried his face into his moist palms. Here he was again, about to come off like some fucking crackpot ... on Crack ... and pot.

"Well, what do you think they are?"

"I ... I'm not exactly sure. That's what I was kinda hoping you could help me to answer."

Dr. Simmons scratched her temple. She peered across the table at him, trying to pry her way into his thoughts, trying to comprehend what was going on inside his head. "And what about the woman?" she dug a little deeper; "I understand that she didn't survive the crash."

"Judith ... Judith Sample ..." his voice trailed off as he shifted anxiously in his seat. He just wanted to rewind back to when the good doctor was pouring him a drink and making small talk.

"Why don't you tell me about her," Dr. Simmons requested, crossing her legs and clasping her hands together.

Zach swallowed nervously, "She was nobody really, just someone I worked with, a friend." He could tell by the expression on her face that Dr. Simmons detected his untruthfulness. "Alright, well maybe she was more than a friend."

"Don't be afraid to open up to me Zach," Dr. Simmons advised. "I need you to be completely honest with me. That's the only way I can help you," she paused for a few awkward moments that allowed reassurance to take verbal form. "Everything you tell me will be kept in the strictest of confidence. Nothing leaves this office. She paused again, then leaned over the table toward him as if ready to spill her own nasty little secret, "And let me tell you, I've heard it all."

Zach felt embarrassed now. He had always been so accomplished when it came to weaving a wool blanket. Or, had it been that Katie was just so gullible? Whatever the case, he knew he wouldn't be able to pull anything over Dr. Simmons' eyes.

"And how does it make you feel that your friend was killed?" she continued, adding just a wisp of emphasis to the word friend.

He didn't want to appear callous, like an unfeeling animal, but he knew he'd better answer truthfully. The doctor would surely read it in his face again if he lied to her. She seemed the type that could read a Royal Flush on the most even of poker faces. She was that good.

"Honestly," he quickly finished the statement in his mind to measure just how cold it would sound; and though it sounded downright frigid, he knew he had to continue, "I guess I felt more relieved than anything. That must sound awful, I don't want to come of like some monster, I mean there was some remorse but …"

Dr. Simmons' expression held staunch, unaffected by the chill of his confession. "The accident was a very traumatic experience, I'm sure," her level response took a professional tone. "It could be that your feelings of guilt and remorse were suppressed from the very beginning, never allowed to surface because of the threat they posed to your recovery, both physically and mentally. These nightmares, hallucinations, whatever we choose to label them, they could very likely be an escape route for those feelings that you have bottled up inside, feelings you may never have even realized you had."

Zach processed the doctor's suggestion which, and Zach was being completely candid with himself, just didn't seem to fit. "I don't know Doc …"

"Did you ever hear of Posttraumatic Stress Disorder?" Dr. Simmons interrupted, and then continued before he was able answer. "The psychological effects of an event as significant as a car accident, especially when someone dies in that accident, can sometimes be as significant as the event itself. It's not at all uncommon for those effects to manifest themselves in various forms, such as depression, anxiety, violent anger, the inability to talk or move for several moments, and quite often, nightmares, or even hallucinations.

Maybe that was it. Maybe Zach wasn't giving himself enough credit. Maybe Judith's death really had affected him much more than he realized, deep down in some unfamiliar place inside. And maybe it was that hidden place that he kept going to when he witnessed all of those horrible things.

"Have you turned to alcohol or drugs since the accident?" Dr. Simmons impeded Zach's thoughts just as he started to convince himself that they might carry some validity.

There it was, the easy answer. Somehow he knew it would come out. It was probably dangling there, right on the tip of her tongue the whole time. Shouldn't she have asked that question before she poured him the glass of scotch?

"No drugs!" he answered swiftly and with a hardened tone. "An occasional wine or a can of beer but … listen, Dr. Simmons, whatever the hell it is that's going on in my skull, I can tell you it has nothing to do with what you're thinking."

"It's not that I think that's the case here Zach," she clarified, noting the sudden tension that stiffened his response. "It's just a standard question; a possibility I had to eliminate is all. Many people in your situation turn to those types of … let's just call them, releases."

"Well, you can definitely eliminate that one," Zach assured firmly. Besides, this woman had absolutely no idea what *situation* he was really in. A few moments of awkward silence passed before he abruptly changed the subject, "This Posttraumatic Stress Disorder, it could make a person see things, feel things that are so real? I mean, when it's happening, I don't feel any different than I do … like right now for example." Zach waved his arms in the air before pinching himself on the back of his right wrist. "And then all of a sudden, bam," he slammed his hand against the leather armrest of his chair, "it's over and I'm right back where I was before it all started."

Dr. Simmons sat with two fingers pressed to the side of her mouth. They pushed her cheeks into an expression of thoughtful deliberation that slipped away after several seconds. "I believe that what you experience during one of your episodes is very similar to what, for example, a veteran of war experiences when they have a flashback. A car backfires and the person believes that it's gunfire. They believe so intently that they act out, sometimes in a very violent manner. They're so convinced, in fact, that they would kill if they felt they had to in order to survive what they perceive as real." Dr. Simmons paused to summarize in her head, "The power of the human mind is such that it can turn fantasy into reality. One's reality is, in reality, nothing more than what one's mind perceives it to be."

Zach was silent. His eyes picked out the empty glass on the table in front of him. For a long moment, he just stared at it. He followed a bead of condensation as it trickled down the etched surface and onto the table. *Drinking. Drugs.* Deep down inside, he wished that could explain why all of this crazy shit was happening. That way, he could just quit and the hallucinations would too.

Chapter Twenty-One

Got milk? Who cares? Four words on a black screen followed by a still shot of a carton labeled CalciYum NonDairy Beverage. Nineteen seconds. That was it. And that was all it needed to be.

The boardroom door swung open with a burst of laughter and praise that sounded off like an alarm through the long, narrow hallways and spacious common areas of Ink Advertising's headquarters. Zach had done it again. His second commercial for the CalciYum account received the advertising industry's equivalent of a five star review. Just as the first one had. And the one for Resurrection Cologne. And just about every other project he had ever attached his creative, sometimes jagged, but always unique perspective onto. Zach's was the type of ingenious mind that could make a paper clip seem like the ideal thing to hold together a valuable report or a classified proposal or even a teetering marriage. Or, at the very least, present that paper clip as the hippest piece of office equipment this side of a voice-activated computer. He had once again validated his artistic superiority and took another step toward reserving his seat at the big table. Only this time, he wasn't smiling, at least not on the inside.

"You've really outdone yourself this time Bell, you truly are gifted. I think maybe it's time we start talking partnership."

"Thank you Mr. Fairfax," Zach paused, "Listen, I need to talk to you about something when you get a minute."

The praise that spilled like CalciYum from Douglas Fairfax would make what Zach had to do that much more difficult. He knew he was the firm's superstar exec, the ace of the staff; he also knew he had to do it, for his own sake, his own sanity.

"Just so happens I have one right now," Fairfax offered in a jovial inflection, "Let's go to my office and you can lay the whole load on me."

Zach tailed the bobbing, and balding, oval man down the hallway that led to the Vice President's office, an office that fifty-nine year old Douglas Fairfax had occupied for the better part of two years.

Zach had to request a leave of absence. *A week? A month?* He wasn't sure. He didn't know how long it would take to pull himself together, or even if he would be able to at all. He only knew that his life was a circus and another major account was a lion he just couldn't tame at the moment. His work would surely suffer and, like any great artist, he couldn't allow that to happen.

Sure, he could probably pull it off ... in their eyes. They would likely see his next project as just another Bell masterpiece. But he would know. He simply didn't have another one in him right now. He wasn't even sure how he had squeezed the CalciYum idea out of his polluted brain; and that one displayed his brilliance in a more Minimalist style. Although, he did have to admit, it was good. Damn good.

After a few seconds, the two men entered what could, with the addition of bedding and shower facilities, be converted into a luxury condo. There was a spacious seating area with a leather sofa and sixty-two inch screen television, a bar stocked with fine imported liquors, a breath swiping panorama of the city, and wall to wall carpeting that even the furniture felt comfortable on. Next to the bar was a ten-foot Christmas tree, white with blue and silver ornaments, and an assortment of holiday do-dads that gave the office the feel of North Pole Command Central.

"Have a seat Zach, make yourself comfortable," Fairfax suggested as he motioned Zach toward the sofa. "I hope there's not some sort of a problem or anything."

Zach gathered his nerve in a deep, stalling breath, "Actually, that's what I wanted to speak to you about. I'm afraid there is."

"Money? Is that the monkey here Bell? Cause if it is ..." Fairfax paced a crocked line behind the sofa. He loosened the tie knot that pressed snug against his Adam's apple, suddenly feeling as nervous as Zach. Could he be loosing the top mind on the staff? Zach was the best damn advertising man in all of New York, as far as he was concerned. Next to himself, of course.

Zach shook his head and waved his hands above it, "No, no, that's not it at all sir. All the money in the Gates giant piggy bank couldn't help me with this problem."

"Family troubles?" Fairfax inquired as he circled around the side of the sofa and into Zach's view. "You and the misses have a falling out or something?" A mask of counterfeit concern stumbled across his face.

"It has nothing to do with Katie or the girls really, at least not directly. I'm kinda alone on this one."

"Drugs? Is that it? You know the company has a wonderful assistance program for that sort of thing. It is completely confidential and ..."

"No, it's not that either sir," Zach interrupted Fairfax's presumptuous rambling. "I wish I were on drugs. Maybe that would explain the whole damn thing."

"I'm not quite sure I follow."

Zach sat quietly for a few moments as cumbersome silence prodded him to explain. He did not want to humor this very intelligent, sapient man with absurd tales of demons and such. He knew he would come across as some irrational fool and couldn't bare the thought of the scarred reputation that most certainly would result; although his reputation did label him as a man with a rather adventurous imagination.

"Dizzy spells," he finally blurted, and then proceeded with the fabrication he had rehearsed the entire drive into town. "It seems like a dozen or more an hour. My head just starts spinning until I'm ready to pass out. I don't know if it's stress or what. I'm quite sure my accident has something to do with it though."

Fairfax's concern grew somewhat genuine now. That concern, however, was more for Zach the crack advertising exec than Zach the human being. "That sounds pretty serious, Bell. Have you consulted a doctor about this dizziness?"

This was it. This was Zach's chance to finish the sale. A lucid version of what would surely seem ridiculous in its true form, especially to a person as grounded as Douglas Fairfax. He had him on the hook. Now, he just had to reel him in. "Yes, as a matter of fact, I have. She said that my problem was not uncommon among people like myself who have endured a tragic experience like an automobile accident." Zach paused for a moment, his mind grasping for some way to end this explanation before he started to sound like a shrink. "She suggested I take it easy for a little while, that's all."

"Well, if that's the good doctor's orders," Fairfax said tentatively, clueless to the fact that "doctor" in this case meant psychiatrist.

"Thank you sir, I really do appreciate it." Zach stood up from the sofa and extended a hand to Fairfax, who had stood throughout the entire conversation. "I just need some time to get my head straight." *Time to get my head straight. Real good, Zach*! Now if that didn't sound like the statement of a person with serious mental issues. "Anyway," Zach continued quickly, hoping to snuff out any suggestions his last statement may have advanced, "I want to thank you for your concern and your understanding Mr. Fairfax. I'll give you a buzz in a few days to let you know how I'm coming along."

"No problem Zach, take as much time as you need," Fairfax yanked the knot of his tie snug against his neck. "Just remember that you're our best man, our numero uno. I need you back at it as soon as you're a hundred percent." Fairfax winked, "Of course, your seventy probably ain't too shabby."

"I'll certainly keep that right here," Zach responded, poking a finger at his left temple as he walked across the room toward the door. "I'm sure I'll be fine in no time."

Fairfax opened his mouth to speak and the expression on his face displayed the insincerity of the advice he was about to offer, "And hey, take it easy. Spend some quality time with your girls, the wife. Don't make the same mistake I did after they opened my chest up last August. My only concern was getting back to this place, getting caught up." He chuckled and his words took on a strong hint of suggestion, "That is, unless of course, you start to miss us."

Zach opened the door and stepped out into the hallway, "Thanks again sir, I'll try and follow that advice." He stood in relief outside the doorway of Fairfax's office. He had just come through lying to the man who signed his paychecks … unscathed.

What had there been to worry about anyway? What would Fairfax have done? Fire the ace of the staff? And besides, he hadn't really been lying, not totally anyway. He really did need the time away and it really was because his head was sick. It was just easier when he didn't have to mix in the truth.

He was left to wonder, however, what the boss had really said to him. Left to decipher the mixed message that dangled from the bald man's fraudulent regard. He knew that Fairfax's single genuine concern was when Zach would be back to pumping out the ideas that pumped in the big bucks.

Fairfax had always been a bottom line guy; his offer to Zach to take as much time as he needed sounded like a man giving advice on his own execution. This was the same man that nearly fired Wicks in Accounting for leaving early the day his wife went into labor. Zach knew, however, that there were a hundred people out there who could crunch numbers like Wicks. He also knew, when it came to making commercials, someone would be hard pressed to find another Zachary Bell. Still, he could interpret the real message in his boss's vocabulary, "You better get your ass back to work real soon."

Chapter Twenty-Two

January 13

A flash of light burst from Katie's camera and Dove's eyes were forced closed, as if by the sun. When they opened once again, the large square box wrapped in Rescue Ranger pink still encumbered her view of Aria, who sat across the table giggling at the playful antics of Perry the Partysaurus. The other seven children seated around the table were also captivated as the hired claw artfully exhaled a zoo of twisted rubber right before their wonder-filled eyes.

Dove, however, seemed more intrigued by the mysterious contents of the box in front of her and began to tug tentatively at the red ribbon that dangled so enticingly from the matching bow.

"Not yet, Sweetie. You have to wait until we sing Happy Birthday."

Dove pulled her tiny fingers away from the package, a slight frown etched into her face, as a child's dose of anxiety swelled up inside her. She knew, however, that she wasn't supposed to open any gifts until after cake and ice cream. That is why she hadn't simply attacked the package the way she would on a full tummy. "When are we gonna sing Happy Birthday, mommy?"

"Yeah mommy, when, when, when? Aria pushed further. "I'm hungry."

The other six children seated around the table joined in the sudden uprising spawned by the birthday girl and her sister and quickly escalating toward a full-fledged tantrum riot.

"As soon as daddy finds the candles ... ZACH!"

"Okay … okay … I've got them, I'm coming." Zach hurried into the kitchen waving a small box over his head like a white flag. The children began to cheer and Perry nailed a few steps of what he called the "Prehistoric Prance." A mutiny had just been averted, narrowly.

"Are there enough?" Katie inquired as Zach hovered over the kitchen table poking candles into the word HAPPY.

"We've got enough here for old Perry's next birthday and he's gotta be pushing a billion."

"I think nine will be plenty." Katie suggested.

"Yeah daddy, it's my birthday, not yours!" Dove proclaimed in a sarcastic tone that seemed to suggest Zach's last birthday cake had resembled a forest fire.

"Very funny young lady." Zach found himself in excellent spirits. In fact, he couldn't remember a time in the last several weeks when his mood was brighter. Nearly a month had passed since his last episode and he had already regained a firm sense of control over his life.

Maybe it was the medication that Dr. Simmons had prescribed or the time away from work. Or, maybe, his subconscious mind had found a way to deal with the guilt and anxiety of his accident and the death of Judith Sample, guilt and anxiety that he didn't even know existed. Dr. Simmons had insisted that recognition was the first step on a long and bumpy road to recovery and even though Zach had yet to recognize anything more than token remorse, it seemed now as if he stood at the cessation of that road.

The nightmares were over. *Nightmares.* That's all they had been really, nothing more than dreams. He knew that now. Maybe he hadn't always been sleeping; but just like Dr. Simmons suggested, one doesn't necessarily have to be physically asleep to dream. He just had to force himself to believe it.

Zach was going back to the office next week and that too was good news. He was certainly looking forward to getting back at it. He missed it, missed being the king. And even that bitch Tiffany Bailey couldn't steal his crown.

He poked colored wax through Double Chocolate Brownie icing like pins through a voodoo doll. In fact, if that slut says one more goddamn word or bats those plastic fucking eyelashes …

"Come on Zach, hurry up with those candles," Katie impeded his vengeful musings, "before Dove's presents get cold."

"Ha ha!" he snickered as he lit each wick with one of those ever so handy butane thing-a-majigs that she handed him from the drawer below the counter. "Is everybody ready now?" He raised his hands above his head like a symphony conductor. "Haaaaaaaaapy Birthday to you …" Zach stared down upon the engaging glow of the candles as he sang. Things were definitely looking brighter.

Chapter Twenty-Three

"MOTHER IN PERU GIVES BIRTH TO LIZARD BOY." Zach always noticed people leafing through the pages of these preposterous tabloids while standing in the checkout line but it seemed as if nobody ever put one in their shopping cart. And why did they always jam the damn thing in the wrong slot when they put it back, in front of People or U.S News and World Report?

"Price check on four," the voice of a teenage girl rang out over the P.A system and pulled Zach's eyes from the article about the baby boy with an iguana's head. He was just like any other child. That was, except for that nasty little habit of capturing dinner on the tip of his tongue as it flew past his grotesquely deformed face.

Zach gazed up at the illuminated register marker. *Checkout four.* It figured! The young lady with the green Food Fair smock and pink-streaked blonde hair stood behind her register holding a bottle of what appeared to be salad dressing in her right hand as she tapped the painted fingernails of her left hand on the automatic pricing scanner. She popped up on the tips of her sneakers and scanned the sales floor in search of whichever acne-scarred stock boy would drag himself to the checkout, retrieve the item of heated debate, and return several minutes later to verify that it was indeed three forty-nine.

Everyone else in line was growing extremely agitated. How dare that customer hold up the line by disputing the price of a lousy bottle of Creamy Caesar's, especially since the bitch had twelve items in the eight-items-or-less express lane? And no, six cans of the same Green Giant sweet corn did not count as one item. So sayeth the unwritten bible of grocery store etiquette.

Zach, on the other hand, was grateful he would have enough time to learn how the lizard boy's skin changed colors in direct sunlight. He quickly recounted the items in his cart. *Only seven.* Four cans of Mighty Dog, a pound of Genoa Salami, Pecan Sandies, and string cheese. As he dropped his head back down into the magazine, he heard the intolerant scowl of the woman in line behind him and the fading whines of her obnoxious toddler who was pleading relentlessly for a Rocket Pop before the damn things were paid for.

Suddenly, he felt the nudge of a metal basket against his hip and snapped his head up. "Hey, why don't you watch ...," his words fell off in mid-sentence. He was unable to see the impatient young mother who had just bumped him with her shopping cart before scooting away to a now open lane six. In fact, he couldn't see anything at all.

It was completely dark around him now. Had there been some sort of a power failure that consumed all the light in the grocery store? No. He knew, somehow, that he was no longer in the Food Fair. This was a much deeper blackness. This was another one of those episodes. Oh shit, not again! This couldn't be happening again. Zach had finally convinced himself that there would be no further episodes. Until now.

The beep of the electronic scanners. The squeal of rusting shopping cart wheels. The muffled chatter of anxious customers. The familiar reality of that oddly comforting chaos was gone, replaced by silence, uncertainty and fear.

The magazine he had held in his hands was gone too, as were the clothes he had been wearing. He was completely naked and standing ... somewhere. He didn't know where. He only knew that it wasn't the grocery store.

A stiff, warm breeze stirred a chorus of shuffling leaves and snapping branches. Zach could feel grains of raw earth under his bare feet. He was quite certain that he was outside. It was, however, no longer winter, at least not where he stood at the moment. Perhaps, he was in the woods somewhere, in a black forest. He could also sense that he was not alone, that someone ... or something ... stood in front of him. It was so dark.

He opened his hands and reached out, poking at the air in blind hesitance in an attempt to identify whatever it was that lingered only a few feet away. The tips of his fingers brushed against what felt like human skin. It was rough and shriveled, but it was human, he hoped. He jerked his hand back quickly. Someone was definitely there in the blackness, a mere arm's length away. "Who's the ... the ... there," he spoke in fear-stuttered fragments.

"My name is Frederick," a gentle voice came at him through the darkness. An unfamiliar voice. The voice of an elderly man. Zach was relieved that it had a name.

"Where am I? What happened to the lights? And what happened to the Food Fair?"

"Food Fair?" the old man chuckled, "I can't say where you are my boy but I sure as hell ain't at no Food Fair. I'm standin in the middle of a beautiful meadow. There are flowers everywhere and the sun is shinin bright and pretty soon, I'm gonna walk through that there door and they're gonna take me to my precious Mary Ann." The joyous voice paused. "You know she's been waitin on me for seven years."

Confusion rattled Zach's brain so vehemently his temples began to throb. Door? What door? And who were *they*? There was no meadow, no flowers, and certainly no sun. What in the hell was this crazy old coot rambling about? Just then, Zach remembered, he was the crazy one. "What in the fuck is happening to me?" he insisted loudly.

"Oh, I understand now," the unseen stranger stated. "You're one of them other fellas, I guess."

"Other fellas? What do you mean, other fellas?" Zach wasn't sure he wanted to know.

"Well, you see son," the old man responded, "there are some

folks here who have stepped from darkness into light. Others, they've stepped from light into darkness. And then, there are those who've been ... let's just say, stumblin around in darkness all along and not even realizin it."

Suddenly, there was light. And a door. *There was a door.* The old man was right. It swung open and a pale flickering light spilled out into the onyx layers of nothingness that had contained them, or at least him. Even though it was a dim light, it stung Zach's eyes closed, but only for a moment. He pried them open just enough to capture a vague image of the old man being escorted down what appeared to be some sort of a tunnel, by what filtered through his narrow slits only as obscure shadows.

Then, almost as quickly as it opened, the door slammed shut again. Once more, darkness was the keeper of the world around him and Zach never caught a glimpse of the structure through which the tunnel led. He only knew that he was next in line to enter. There was nobody else in front of him. But there were others behind. He could feel them there, hear them breathe, smell their trepidation. Not all of them were happy to be there like the old man. Something sinister awaited them inside. *Awaited him!*

He tried to speak. Terror strangled his words. He wanted to run. He was unable. His legs were as stiff as two-by-fours and the darkness restrained him like a straight jacket. These dreams, hallucinations, whatever they were, they did not allow him to flee, to escape, at least not until they released him.

Once again, Zach stood in blackness and, once again, he fumbled without sight in search of some clue. What was it that he would soon enter? A building perhaps? He could make out the wooden door through which the old man entered and, as his hands explored further, they scraped across what felt like stone ... cold and rigid. A cave? Not likely. The structure was too defined, at least parts of it man-made. What he felt was a wall.

Zach could only wait. To die? To be ushered through another dimension of a place that exists beyond the boundaries of reality, then spit back out into that reality, confused and terrified? He wasn't sure. What he was certain of was that his insanity was being validated further.

A chill crept across his bare skin and yet, the anticipation soaked him with sweat. That door would open again very soon. And then, it did.

* * *

Crude and unpolished, an obscenely macabre replica of the opera houses that peppered midtown Manhattan—that was Zach's impression of the vast space in which he now found himself. Only here, the audience was not a gathering of tuxedo-attired gentlemen and their diamond-embellished wives. Here, as he stood on a large stage of unfinished wood, he peered into an assembly of robed spectators. They seemed, in their silence, to anticipate some ... performance.

To his left, seated in ascending rows of wood-plank benches, were hundreds of black shrouded figures, segregated from those on the right, those in white, by a wide aisle that extended to the arched exits behind them. Their entire forms, including their faces, were concealed under the hooded cloaks that harbored individual identity. On each of their laps was something that loosely resembled an index card glued to a tongue depressor. Zach could feel their hidden eyes upon him as stony walls held the chill of their secret stares.

Dust-laden curtains of red linen had been drawn to either side of the stage and a haunting chandelier of bones and candles cast an eerie glow from the sloped ceiling high above.

But why? Why was he here? What was his purpose? His role? A jester to the royal court of some unearthly kingdom? The actor in a solo showcase of suffering?

Would this sinister Swan Lake be his swan song?

He waited. Fear softened his stance, almost to the point of collapse. *And waited.* His heartbeats were so relevant, he could actually hear them. *And waited.* For what, he wasn't certain.

A man's voice, ominously baritone, demanded all attention as it echoed through the hollow auditorium, amplified either by some hidden speaker system or by the sheer flatulence of the air. "Next on the block, the soul of one Zachary Bell."

The block? What block? Oh god, not a chopping block. But it wasn't a chopping block. An auction, that's what this was. An auction of souls? Zach shuttered at the implication. Was this it? Had death finally found him, nestled in the tiny crevasses of his madness? Or had that madness found yet another torture to inflict upon him?

If he were indeed dead, he could not recall how the end had claimed him. He was certain, however, that he did not want to be ... sold ... to those in black. The evil from that side of the room was substantial, so heavy it seemed to throw the entire auditorium out of balance.

"The bidding will open at one thousand Runes," the unseen auctioneer instructed.

All of those on the left side of the auditorium, those in the black robes, raised their cards over their hooded heads. Only one in white did the same. *One!* Zach was doomed already.

"Two thousand."

Several of the black shrouded figures lowered their cards.

"Three thousand."

Other arms dropped. The bidder in white, however, held firm. Zach clinched his hands into tight fists, silently urging the bidder in white. Please, whatever he means by runes, bid ten thousand if you must, twenty.

"Four thousand."

Only two bidders remained now, one amongst the black clad figures and the one in white.

"Five thousand Runes."

One card was lowered, one remained raised.

"Five thousand once ... five thousand twice ... sold ... to the bidder in the last row."

The bidder in white had prevailed. Relief crutched the crippling fear that had threatened to drop Zach right where he stood. White was goodness, purity. It was the ones in black that he should dread, the ones in black that were sent from Hell, right?

The white-shrouded form rose up from the bench. The others remained still, preserved in anonymity. Its gloved fingers came slowly up to the hood that guarded its mystery and as it was pulled back, terror once again seized Zach. This was indeed the unveiling of purity … pure evil.

A face was revealed, a human face. But then again, not human at all. It was the face of Judith Sample, concealed behind the mask that death had assigned her. She was a pale, lifeless semblance of the woman he had once looked upon with such adoration, such lust. Her eyes were as black as the cloaks of those who sat across the aisle from her. Her lips moved not to speak, only to smile; and when they did, her pallid skin, bleached in death and spoiled by sin, started to rupture.

Zach dropped to a knee as blood, red as the blood that warms the living, began to seep from the cracks that stretched across her expression of morbid delight. It stained the ivory cloak that still shrouded whatever abomination remained concealed below the collar.

Suddenly, Zach heard a surrendering creek. He felt a shimmy, then a jerk. The stage on which he knelt began to splinter and break apart. He reached for something, anything to grab onto as wood separated from wood beneath him, slivers peeling away from each other like string cheese.

There was nothing to cling to and he dropped between the jagged planks. The earth did not stop him. It had, in fact, opened itself to swallow him. He continued to plummet. Oxygen was yanked from his lungs and his stomach felt as if it was being wrenched inside out. He closed his eyes as the hems of the earth's gut whisked upward in a vertical rush, stifling his desperate screams. This had to be the end. He was falling to Hell.

Then, all at once, his seemingly endless descent came to an abrupt halt, though he hadn't hit the ground.

"Noooooo," his voice dried up. He opened his eyes in cautious protest. A familiar scene unraveled around him. Pepsi coolers. Shopping carts. Produce scales.

"Hey buddy, what the hell's wrong with you? You gonna check out or what? My days are ticking away here!" Zach turned to an old woman who had inched her way up beside him. She was wearing yellow sweatpants and a green coat and balancing seven cartons of Newports in her arms. Her thick tangled wig of unruly curls gave her the appearance of Medusa with a home-perm. "Let's go, I ain't got all frickin year, either crap or get off the pot!"

Zach thought he had already checked out ... permanently.

"Sir, you're next," the cashier motioned him forward impatiently.

He did not respond. He trampled the tabloid magazine that had fallen to the floor at his feet as he trudged out of line toward the exits, leaving his shopping cart to block the aisle.

"Sir, your groceries, sir, don't you want ..." The girl with the pink streaked hair shook her head and chuckled, "What a head case!"

Zach dragged himself unevenly past rows of cashiers and grocery baggers and toward the electronic doors that peeled away from the brisk walls of winter. He walked, totally oblivious, into a cart stacked with unassembled Sunday papers. He stepped clumsily around it, and then proceeded without direction through the exit doors. He was oblivious to the chill just beyond those doors, but not to the chill within himself ... within his soul.

Chapter Twenty-Four

5:23 P.M.

Counciling. Pills. What was next, a lobotomy? Zach had known all along that he would be back to see Dr. Simmons. This appointment had been scribbled in the books during his last session.

But this time would be different. Or, so he had come to believe. This time he would tell the good doctor that he no longer required her services. She was his savior, a guardian angel, but everything was fine now and he wouldn't need her hanging around on his shoulder anymore. At a hundred bucks a clip, that was certainly a pricey halo that floated over her head.

A million dollars. Ten million. Whatever the price. Zach was now willing to pay any amount. He would rob a hundred banks to get the cash. If only it would all go away. If only there was a price tag for sanity, used or otherwise.

But Zach knew that he would not be able to buy back his lucidity and even if he could, he hadn't the slightest idea what store to shop. He sure as hell hoped that Dr. Simmons did.

* * *

5:40 P.M.

"From a single delicate strand comes an intricate inescapable web." The voice was a whisper, not of timid apprehension or undiscovered purpose, but of conviction, unwavering and deliberate. The words were spoken in a delicate tone and yet, the message would have been no more profound in its reception had it been delivered on a thousand decibels.

Zach whipped his head around in an attempt to locate Cheryl Simmons, who stood behind him only moments before. He was certain; however, that it was not her voice he had just heard. His eyes cased the rear of the office that filtered untarnished over the back of his seat. Who was there?

"Go ahead Zach, continue," Dr. Simmons instructed, "I'm still here."

Dr. Simmons sat in the chair across from him and the sound of her voice brought his eyes forward again. She had not been in the chair when he turned away, but she was there now. And she was not behind him. And it was not her voice that had pulled his attention that way. And he was overcome with bewilderment and fear.

"Did you hear someone?" He already knew the answer.

"What do you mean?" she inquired, her expression gathering youthful skin in wrinkles of concern.

"Talking ... just a few seconds ago"

"Only you," she answered. "You were telling me about standing in line at the grocery store and then ..."

"And then I heard her voice," he interrupted.

"Voice?"

"You're witnessing a little piece of my fucking insanity right now Doc and I bet you didn't even know it."

As the sound of the whispered message replayed in his mind, its source became terrifyingly clear to him. "Judith ... it was Judith Sample again."

"Your misdeeds have snared you like a helpless moth and I am the spider who shall feast upon your entangled carcass."

There it was again. Only this time it was closer, so close he could feel Judith's breath on his earlobe. The muscles in his neck constricted as he leapt up from his chair. Terrified, he spun around once again, frisking the atmosphere with swollen sight. And once again, nothing.

"She's here! Judith is here!" Zach turned slowly back toward Dr. Simmons. "She is in this room, right now!"

"No, Zach," the doctor assured as she seductively unsnapped the top button on her blouse, "it's only you and me in this room right now. You just need to forget all about Judith Sample. Just pretend she's your wife."

"What are you doing?"

"I think I've figured out what your problem is Zach, and I know just the treatment for it." Dr. Simmons unsnapped the second button, then the third. A naked, swollen nipple peeked out through the soft material of her blouse as the options played through Zach's mind like a movie listing.

Something didn't feel right about this whole thing. It had nothing to do with guilt, however, and everything to do with fear. Once again, he had heard the voice of a dead woman and he could still feel her presence, still smell her death all around him.

Dr. Simmons pulled one arm from her blouse. "I've wanted you from the moment you walked into this office." The blouse fell from her shoulder onto the carpeted floor.

Zach wanted to run. He didn't want to run. He wasn't sure. He was frightened. He was aroused. He was both. That's what made it so exciting. That's what kept him there. The halogen lamp across the room dimmed to a candle's glow. *Bad wiring.* Zach remembered what Dr. Simmons had told him about the wiring the last time he was here. Now, however, he did not believe it.

Dr. Simmons strutted around the table that separated her from her patient. Her breasts were firm and attentive. Her eyes, scorched with lust. She reached out to embrace Zach as he fell back into his chair. Suddenly, he wasn't thinking about Judith anymore. Or his wife.

"Don't worry," Dr. Simmons advised as she straddled his leg and allowed the slight quiver of his left hand to massage her breast, "I'm the doctor and I'm going to take very good care of you."

Zach could feel the moist warmth of her desires through his

pant leg and the wet passion of her open mouth as she sealed it over his. Their eyes closed and their tongues explored. Zach could no longer contain the fire ignited by the doctor's curious fingers, a fire that could only be extinguished in the flood of his own concupiscence or …

Suddenly, Zach could feel his tongue being drawn farther into Dr. Simmons' mouth. *Too far.* His cheeks collapsed and his nostrils struggled for oxygen. It seemed as if she was trying to suck his soul right out of him, up through his throat like soda through a straw. His eyes opened as he grasped her shoulders firmly, trying to push her away as he pulled his own head back. He could not free himself. He could not separate his mouth from hers and his guts trembled as if the suction from their kiss would tug his stomach right out through his mouth.

Just as the final currents of lust drained into a whirlpool of panic, Dr. Simmons released her lip lock. But only for a moment, barely enough time for what tasted like realization to settle into Zach's unsettled stomach. It wasn't Dr. Simmons who now straddled him. It was Judith. He knew it was Judith who had been whispering to him on the foul breath of his insanity, who was once again assaulting him from someplace deep inside his own darkening existence.

She appeared normal, in the glow of a beauty that life's brightest light had once cast upon her. *Normal, except for the vengeance in her eyes.* The flames of that eternal inferno from which she had once again emerged scorched her gaze with what seemed like all the hate in Hell. Zach lost that gaze as Judith pulled his face back to hers. He tried to resist. He could not. She was much too powerful. He tried to push her from his lap. It was like pushing against the side of Madison Square Garden.

Scrambled thoughts of fear and desperation wrestled with the chaos in his mind. He had to keep his mouth closed, no matter what. His jaws locked as Judith pressed her lips to his. He nearly screamed. *Mouth closed,* he remembered.

Judith became enraged at his resistance, so much so that she sunk her teeth into the flesh of his chin and lower lip. He could feel the pressure as she bit into delicate nerves. The pain was being injected like venom from the fangs of a cobra. He tried to pull away. The pain deepened. It was now unbearable. A sudden burst of raw survival instinct took over.

With a tightly clinched fist and the adrenaline of a cornered animal behind it, Zach landed a right that met Judith's jaw with enough force to knock her from his lap. The weight of twenty men stuffed into a meager one hundred ten-pound frame, crashed to the floor. Zach sprang up from the chair before she was on top of him again.

Just then, the office door announced its opening with a screech of its hinges and Zach twisted around to find a portly man in his sixties standing just outside. The man appeared, from the dingy leather boots and gray, grease-stained overalls he wore, to be one of the building's maintenance workers.

"What the hell's going on in here?" the man stepped forward into the office to get a better view. "Dr. Simmons, you okay?"

Dr. Simmons? Zach glanced down toward the floor where the doctor teetered on one knee, flexing her left jaw and cradling her chin in her right palm.

"Shit!" Zach reached down and placed a hand under her left arm. "I'm so sorry I ... I ..."

Dr. Simmons jerked angrily out of his grip.

"I'm calling security!" the old man at the door warned as he backed swiftly into the hallway. "Don't you go nowhere!"

Zach's concern for the doctor turned inward, "But she attacked me!" He pondered that accusation for a moment before continuing in an unsteady voice, "Well, I guess it wasn't her." His face became flush with disconcertion as he fell back down into his chair.

"No, no Carl, it's okay," Dr. Simmons called out to the old man who had started toward the service phone at the end of the hall.

A few seconds later, he reappeared outside the door. "You sure about that, Doc?"

Dr. Simmons, who now stood unevenly, bracing herself against the armrest of her chair, peered at her pitiful client slouched down in his. She had to remain committed to the welfare of her patient. "Yes, Carl, I'll be fine. Don't worry about it."

"Alrighty," Carl plucked a flashlight from his rear pant's pocket and brandished it like a Billy Club out in front of him. "You need me, you scream. I'll only be a couple doors down fixing the air conditioning. It's been down since fall and the hot weather's nearly on us again."

"Thanks Carl, I'll be okay."

As Carl peeled away from the door he deliberately left open, a dense, uneasy silence rushed into the office.

Dr. Simmons towed herself over to the cabinet behind her desk. She pulled out a glass and filled it to the rim with ice cubes, then baptized the ice with Scotch from a half empty bottle she had also retrieved from the cabinet.

"Scotch?" she offered, breaching the quiet as she reached for a second glass.

Zach did not answer and her fingers stopped a few inches short of the glasses in the cabinet, eagerly returning to her own. She pulled it up to her face, took a sip, then placed it cautiously on the bruise that had already began to swell and discolor her lower cheek.

"What happened?" the words fell from Zach's bloody lip like baby drool.

Dr. Simmons walked back across the room and sat down in the chair across from him. "You don't know, do you?" she asked, waiting for the answer she already knew.

Zach just shook his head.

"Well, we were discussing yesterday afternoon … the grocery store. You asked me if I heard something … looked behind you … a few seconds later you tightened up … your entire body, you started squirming around in the chair and then …"

"And then, I socked you," Zach finished.

Dr. Simmons took another sip from her glass, then returned it to her swollen jaw.

"The expression on your face, you were terrified of something. I walked over, started shaking you. Next thing I know, I'm on the floor."

Zach put his finger up to his mouth. The blood on his lower lip had already begun to crust. "What about my lip?"

"You must have bit it or something, when you were thrashing around."

"So we never … kissed?"

She chuckled, a reaction not of humor but of surprise, "Kissed? No!"

"And I guess it's safe to assume you didn't see my deceased ex-girlfriend kissing me either?"

Dr. Simmons twirled her glass in her hand and stared down into the mini whirlpool of ice and alcohol that spun like the thoughts in her head. She wasn't quite sure how to tell Zach what she had just come to realize in that very instant.

She had always been straight forward with all of her patients, and even though she had never attempted to tighten a screw as loose as this one, she knew that the best bet was to just come right out and say it. "Zach, I have to be honest with you. I'm not really sure I can help you. I think you need to see someone that can offer you a little more in-depth attention."

Zach closed his eyes and dropped his chin against his chest. At that moment, whatever hope he clung to, whatever optimism he dangled from, snapped like a yo-yo constructed of thread and brick. He was too fucked up for even the best shrink an honest dollar could buy. Sanity simply could not be bribed. "What exactly are my options here, Doc? What am I going to do now?"

"Well, there is a place a little north of the city, a clinic …"

"A looney bin," Zach interrupted. He remembered Father Kazcmarek, his final days spent in such a dismal place. It had not been a haven, a sanctuary, for the priest. It had been a trap.

"They're excellent doctors," she explained. "They can perform treatments that I am neither trained for nor equipped to perform."

"What, shock therapy?"

"They've helped a lot of people. I believe they can help you too." It was obvious by her tense demeanor that Dr. Simmons didn't just recommend this "clinic" to every Tom, Dick, and Harry who walked into her office with an over-active id or a propensity for side-stepping reality. Zach could also sense in her tone that she wasn't exactly tossing out a suggestion for him to juggle around for a few days.

"So what, you're going to commit me?"

"Believe me Zach," she assured, "I really don't want to do that. I was kinda hoping you would volunteer to check yourself in. I guess you can take it as a stern recommendation."

Zach was well aware that Dr. Simmons could have him arrested for assaulting her, even though it wasn't her he had meant to strike. He was also aware that the person he had meant to hit has been sharing tight quarters with earthworms for nearly five months. If ever a proposal had some conviction behind it, the one Dr. Simmons offered certainly did.

"Alright," he agreed in feeble hesitation, "give me the information, I'll call first thing tomorrow morning."

Zach retreated back into the thick black mud of his own thoughts as the doctor thumbed through her rolodex in search of the number for the clinic. Maybe he did belong in a nut house. What other option had all of this chaos left him? Once again, Father Kazcmarek invaded his mind. He could think of only one.

Chapter Twenty-Five

So this is it. This is how it's all going to end. It has to be. It can't go on any longer. Zach held the pistol snug in his right palm. His finger discovered the trigger with hesitant strokes. Death was cold in his grip and yet, it conformed without flaw to the contour of his hand. This death, it seemed, had been tailored to him like a custom suit.

Zach had felt the tension of a loaded pistol only once before. When he and his brother Matt were still pre-acne snot noses, father allowed them to fire off a shot of his 9mm into a cardboard ten point in the woods behind Uncle Ricky's farm. Zach was ten. Matt, twelve. Dad had dubbed the event their initiation into manhood. Some man! Zach cried when the forceful kick and deafening bang nearly caused him to relieve himself where he hadn't in over four years. He never cared much for guns after that.

Funny how, more than two decades later, the desperate arms of insanity would reach for the very thing that frightened him as a child, the thing he refused to have in the house until two years ago when a Peeping Tom scared Katie so indelibly, she couldn't sleep a wink for days. Mojo was a feisty little guardian but certainly not the keeper of well being a loaded .38 turned out to be.

Zach was alone, huddled in a chair at the kitchen table. Katie and the girls were somewhere else. He wasn't sure where. Katie had told him where they were going. Her words had been little more than background noise. She had asked him if he was all right and he must have convinced her that he was. He vaguely remembered nodding.

Now! Zach pulled the barrel up to his lips. It had the bitter, metallic taste of a gun that had never been fired. Death, he knew, was not the flavor of cotton candy.

There were no lights on in the house, but the spotlight above the garage door traced his sullen silhouette on the window in front of him. The shadowy profile, suspended for a long moment in the rigid pose of its intentions, relaxed.

Zach plucked the .38 from his mouth as he rocked in the still chair. The sour flavor of the barrel remained on his lips as they peeled from the chilled metal like dry paint. He summoned a deep breath of what he hoped would be courage, then quickly brought the pistol back up to his mouth. His tongue was still sore and swollen from the incident at Dr. Simmons' office and the scab on his lip had not yet formed against the moistness of his saliva. The pain nagged him with the conviction of his madness but the confusion of its origin throbbed much more incessantly than the pain itself.

He pulled the gun away again. He pressed it into the sweat that dampened his right temple. If he was going to pull the trigger, it damn well better get the job done. If he was going to pull the trigger. If he *could* pull the trigger.

He squeezed his eyes shut. Every muscle in his body was bronzed in a plaster of sordid emotion. He was so tense that it felt as if his skin had shrunk around his bones. His left eyelid began to twitch and the pressure inside his head rang constant in his ears.

He lowered the gun once more. And trembled. The sweatshirt he wore did nothing to warm him, for the chill that shook him came not from the air around him, but from deep within his soul. Was he more afraid of taking his own life or of the possibility he might not be able to?

He had to do it. He had to find the guts to pull the trigger. The burden of his madness had become too heavy and the only escape, the only medicine, it seemed, was a bullet in the brain.

He raised the pistol to his temple again. It seemed much heavier this time and he struggled against the increased weight. Was it just in his mind? Maybe it was the swelling burden of fear that fed his corpulent indecision. What if the bullet did not finish him completely? Impossible! A bullet to the brain surely would not fail him.

Or, maybe it was the gravity of guilt that pulled at his arm ... and his brain. He could not do it here, not in the house, at the kitchen table, where he had shared so many dinnertime stories with Dove and Aria.

"Someplace else. Someplace away from here," Zach mumbled aloud to no one as he rose up from the chair and stumbled across the kitchen. He retrieved his keys with the gold Mercedes emblem key chain from the counter and opened the door that led down to the garage. A gust of chilled, musty air stirred his disheveled hair as he stood for a moment at the top of the stairs. Then, like a death row inmate whose eviction notice had just been effected, he took each step with reluctant hesitation, subconsciously savoring the crude sensation of walking ... *for the final time.*

He continued in stocking feet across the cold concrete of the garage toward his car. Without deliberation, he pressed the automatic lock release on his key chain and the command was met with a unified click. In Zach's ears, the click fell in eerie silence, undistinguished, a mere trigger's click against the crack of a loaded gun.

Zach opened the car door. He tossed the loaded .38 across the center console and onto the passenger's seat before dropping down onto the stiff tan leather. He pulled the door shut and pushed a button on the small gray box on the visor at his forehead. The grinding gears of the garage door groaned as it opened slowly. The docile purr of fine German engineering joined in at a turn of the gold ignition key. Zach noticed neither. He could hear only the blast of spent gunpowder, over and over, as the drama of his intentions unfolded in his mind. *Bang!* He flinched and struck his head on the padded headrest behind him. He let out a deep gasp as he stared at the pistol on the seat.

After a long, empty moment, he shifted the tranny into reverse and eased the Mercedes down the driveway onto Crabtree. Through force of habit, he pressed the button on the gray box once again and watched as the closing door eclipsed the light of the vacant garage.

The pistol again pulled Zach's gaze to the passenger's seat. As he started slowly down Grouse Run, he forced his vision forward once more, staring out through the frosty film that began to glaze the windshield. Where would he go? Where was an appropriate place to take one's own life?

"It doesn't matter where you go," a voice answered his mute thoughts from the seat where Katie would often petition him to slow down or watch for crossing deer.

Even though the speedometer barely threatened fifteen, Zach trampled on the brake pedal as if he were once again gaining on the hillside above the Hadley farm at well over forty. He lurched forward slightly, and then settled back against his seat, jamming the gearshift into park.

The Mercedes sat in the middle of the road as the night took shape around it, unclaimed by the lights of a specialty plastics factory a few miles off to the east. "What the fuck do you want now?" he scowled. "Can a man not even kill himself in peace?"

The familiar voice answered, "You cannot kill yourself at all Zachary. It is not in his plan."

"His plan?" Zach turned to Father Kazcmarek, who sat next to him in the passenger's seat inspecting the loaded pistol with mild amusement.

"Nice choice anyway. I wish I could have gotten my hands on one of these while I was in that zoo." The priest chuckled as he put the cold chrome barrel to his temple, "Would have been a hell of a lot smoother than charging a damn wall, that's for sure."

Zach reached over and snatched the gun from Kazcmarek's bony fingers, "I am going to kill myself. I'm going to kill myself right now. You did it and now it's my turn." Zach raised the gun to his head and squeezed his eyes shut. As his finger caressed the virgin trigger, his hand again began to shake.

"Go ahead," Kazcmarek chided. "Go ahead and pull."

Zach took a soliciting breath. His hand trembled so erratically he was unable to hold the end of the barrel in place against his skull.

"The life you live is no longer yours to take."

He could not squeeze the trigger either. What his mind begged his finger refused. He wanted simply to surrender to the insanity. He could not raise the white flag.

"It's not his plan."

"Shut up and get out of my car!" Zach scolded as he slammed his hand against the steering wheel in frustrated rage. "I said out … now!" He turned the gun toward the priest, "Now!"

"It seems that you still do not understand Zachary. But you will, very soon."

Zach lowered the gun to his lap. "Alright then, I'm getting out and don't you fucking follow me."

Zach wrapped his fingers around the door handle but the locks snapped down with a simultaneous "click." He poked repeatedly at the auto-lock button on the console beside him but the locks would not release. He attempted to force the door open, pushing desperately before thrusting his elbow against it. The door would not budge. "Let me …" he whipped his head angrily around to the passenger's side and his words faded.

Kazcmarek was drawing something with his finger on the canvas of frosty breath that clung to the inside of the windshield. Zach starred, entranced, as his abbreviated demand became part of that canvas. A pentagram. Roman numerals, IX, I, III. The image was one he had seen before. It had frightened him. Oddly, more than any other he had ever dreamed, ever hallucinated. It frightened him now, even more. It harbored some dark meaning he had not yet come to realize, a veiled significance he had yet to uncover. *An omen.*

"Very soon," Kazcmarek warned.

Suddenly, the door locks popped up, "click." Zach tugged on the handle and the car door swung open, pulling him out onto the jagged gravel road. He scrambled clumsily to his feet, retrieving the gun that had fallen to the ground, then stumbled forward and began to run. He did not shut the door or grab the keys from the ignition and he wasn't slowed by the pain of sharp rocks jabbing at the tender skin of his shoeless feet. He just wanted to get away from Kazcmarek. If he could only escape the old man's custody, maybe he could end this harassment and amputate himself from the torso of this torment once and for all.

The lights from the plastics plant illuminated his retreat into a thick cluster of trees and brush at the side of the road. The priest didn't follow and Zach never glanced back over his shoulder. He never noticed that Kazcmarek was no longer in the car; that he had simply evaporated. The message had been delivered; the message Zach ignored as he trampled ice coated branches that snapped like insect bones under his soiled socks.

Zach ran until he lost the road completely and stopped. Factory light scattered in random, indefinite swatches against the color of night but the prickly shadows from the refuge of mature pines and naked oaks embraced his solitude. This was the place.

He clutched the loaded pistol in his numb fingers and gagged on the frigid air that strangled his throat and lungs. He could no longer feel the chilled steel in his hand and gazed down to verify that it was still there. It was. And so were his intentions.

Only the nocturnal creatures concealed by nature's camouflage were in his company now. He felt more alone at this moment than he ever had before. Now he could do what he had set out to do. It was only he and the raving madness that had ushered him here to the deathly calm of the woods, the raving madness that seemed to once again extend an offer of silence. The lethal silence of suicide.

Zach put the barrel of the gun to his head. A frozen branch fell from a tree behind him, severed by the weight of winter's cruel unraveling. As it fell to the frost-hardened dirt below, Zach reflected on how he too had come apart, limb by limb, thought by intolerable thought, until he could no longer bare the weight of his mind's own cruel unraveling.

He closed his eyes and his mind. He pulled the door shut on the world and then ... he pulled the trigger. There was a soft click but no bang. He waited for the cold rush of death, the blackness of finality. Neither came. He pulled the trigger again, and again, there was only a slight, empty "click." His eyes opened, slow and reluctant, to the same gray existence he hoped to leave behind.

For a long time, several misplaced minutes, he only stood there frozen in callous disregard of his surroundings. His labored breath took the form of cold reality on the chilled night air. He was indeed still breathing. He was indeed still alive.

Finally, he clicked open the chamber of the pistol still clenched in his right hand. Six shells, unspent. He closed the chamber again and held the gun out in front of him. With the barrel pointed into the darkness, he squeezed the trigger. Bang!

Kazcmarek was right. Zach couldn't kill himself. That reality again took form in his mind and the weight of it dropped him to his knees. The pistol slipped from his grasp as he began to sob uncontrollably.

He was a broken man, choking on the dementia his mind was force feeding him, unable to spit it out. Whatever it was that had a hold on him, whatever it was that had him trapped in the jagged claws of his own insanity, it would eventually kill him itself. It was already peeling his existence away slowly, layer by layer, and enjoying it.

Chapter Twenty-Six

Zach sat slumped in a chair at the kitchen table, his vacant stare forged into the wall. A blue terrycloth blanket was wrapped loosely around his shoulders but it did not subdue the tremors that shook him every few seconds. The coins in the pocket of his pants clamored annoyingly as he shuffled his legs back and forth. He didn't notice.

Katie, who was now at the front door issuing a final thanks to the patrolman for escorting her husband home, had dispatched Dove and Aria to their room.

A passing motorist had called police on her cell phone after spotting Zach's Mercedes in the middle of the road, running in park with its lights on and the door wide open.

The officer found Zach in the road, a few hundred yards from the vehicle, crooked steps taking him aimlessly in the opposite direction. He wasn't wearing shoes or a coat and there was dirt embedded into the knees of his torn trousers. Zach told the officer he had been searching for Mojo and became disoriented when he lost his footing and fell in the woods where he thought he had heard the dog barking. There was no alcohol on his breath and nobody heard the shot he had fired off in the woods, so the officer had no reason to arrest him.

If the officer had taken him in, he would have been trapped in some damp holding cell. There he would have been easy prey. And he was certain that Satan would not post a bond of mercy and just kill him off quickly. The more that Zach thought about it, however, the more he realized that it would have made no difference if he had been locked up. He was already a prisoner, and the cell that contained him was his tormented life.

The officer rode Zach home in his squad car and called a tow truck for the Mercedes. He was, although not intoxicated, obviously in no condition to drive.

Katie came into the kitchen and took a seat next to Zach at the table. The puzzled expression on her face suggested both concern and confusion. The police officer had been skeptical of Zach's story about the dog, especially when Mojo greeted their arrival at the front door with a barrage of barked warnings. Still, he had no cause to take him into custody. Katie, on the other hand, knew for certain that her husband's tale was a total fabrication. "Mo was here the entire time, wasn't he? No shoes or coat and ... and your pants ... what in the world were doing out there sweetie?"

Zach didn't respond. He didn't even move. He only sat there, staring.

"What's the matter with you?" Katie placed her left hand on his shoulder. Still, there was nothing. "Please Zach, talk to me."

For a few moments, he remained entrenched in a numbing, almost peaceful void. But then, against a silent, diluted resistance, a rush of thought scattered those scraps of serenity across the returning clusters of hopelessness and dread.

Zach felt hollow, as if his soul had been sucked out through every pore in his skin, from every corner of his being. Whatever it was that now governed his existence had shoved its infinite arms down his throat and pulled him inside out, then devoured the marrow of his exposed being, morsel by morsel.

Zach lowered his head and closed his eyes. In a weak, defeated voice, he mumbled something Katie could not make out.

"What baby? I couldn't understand you."

He shook his head, laughing sarcastically through his nostrils as he blurted out pieces of his disturbed deliberation, "Couldn't do it, he wouldn't let me do it, wouldn't let me, just wouldn't let me."

"Wouldn't let you what, Zach?" Katie probed. "Who wouldn't let you?"

"Satan, I presume," he began to explain in the most distressed tone she had ever heard from his now quivering lips. "Just couldn't let me end it all. I guess he's having too much fun right now."

The words her delusional husband spilled filtered through Katie like acid. She was unable to respond, nearly unable to breathe, at least for the moment. She realized in that instant what Zach was doing in the woods. Somehow she knew ... her husband had attempted to kill himself. The dreams or hallucinations or whatever the hell they were, they had pushed him completely over the edge.

Katie realized something else as well. She had to be strong right now, as strong as she had ever been in her life, even though she was as scared as she had ever been. Scared of what he might do to himself. To her. To the girls. This man she had been married to for a decade's worth of better or worse had never been worse. Whatever had gotten into him could bust out at any moment. The passive trembling could suddenly erupt into a full-blown quake.

Still, Katie knew what she had to do. "That's it! I'm calling that clinic that Dr. Simmons told you about. I'm calling and you're going, tonight!" She awaited Zach's refusal but he offered no verbal resistance. "Did you hear me, Zach? I'm taking you there tonight."

Nothing. Maybe he didn't hear her. Maybe it simply didn't matter anymore. He sat in silence, lost, perhaps abandoned, in a world he could not explain, a world that was no longer his oyster. Katie could sense the surrender in her husband's placid tone. She was afraid that he might be dying right there in that chair, if not physically, in every other way a person can die.

"I'm calling my sister to watch the kids and then I'm calling the clinic." She paused with one hand on the telephone receiver, "The number's upstairs in the bedroom. You stay right there in that chair and don't move."

Zach remained in a posture of resignation, the same posture he had held for the last twenty minutes. He truly felt as if he wouldn't make it through this thing. His mind … his thoughts … they were being controlled by something much more powerful than himself, something he was certain was not a dream. Maybe that's how it had introduced itself but now, now it was so much more. Now it was a disease, a cancer that had spread through him, eating away at his soul, leaving behind the fat and the gristle. *Leaving him to die.*

Suddenly, there was a loud crash outside the window. It jolted Zach back into reality. Or had it pulled him from it? He broke from his sullen pose. Thunder. That's all it was. A second rumble confirmed its identity. And then came the chorus of pounding rain that followed. Nothing more than a thunderstorm.

But … it was February … *in New York.* Zach hoisted himself out of the chair and started toward the window. It must be ten degrees outside. How in the hell could it be raining?

But it was indeed rain that pelted the frosty glass of the window and pounded the shingled roof above. As he gazed out the window at the freakish weather that had encapsulated the house, weather that he wished he could convince himself was simply a product of global warming, a reflection of light bounced back at him off the glass. The light dimmed and he turned around. There were voices too. And laughter. Someone was in the living room.

Zach walked hesitantly through the kitchen. The pulse of the television was easily recognizable as it pulled him toward it. A feeling of uneasiness tangled with curiosity and wrapped itself around him like straggled roots. Why was television on now? The children were supposed to be in bed and Katie, hadn't she said something about making a phone call?

He turned the corner into the living room and saw Katie and the girls on the sofa. He threw a quick glance at the television and watched as the image of a news reporter standing in front of the White House vanished behind little costumed children adjusting their tails and brushing fur from their tiny faces.

"Katie!" Zach called as he walked up behind the sofa. "Katie!" There was no response.

"Girls?"

Aria spoke, but not to Zach, "Too bad Daddy isn't here to watch me be Nala."

"Maybe he's watching from heaven," said Dove, who was seated next to her sister on the sofa.

Katie and the girls started to laugh sarcastically. "I very much doubt that," Katie chuckled. "And besides, he never was much for keeping promises."

Where had he heard those words before? Those *exact* words? A sharp feeling of deja vu offered a suggestion that seemed preposterous. It was, however, a suggestion he couldn't deny. This exact moment had already come and gone. He was not able to recall it exactly in his memory, but he was certain of it. And now, he was in that moment once again. He just couldn't remember ...

Suddenly, the Cuckoo clock on the wall began to screech. Seven times. Seven o'clock. Seven o'clock! The dream he had in the hospital, right before he had emerged from his coma. That's where he was, inside that first nightmare. Or was it a hallucination? Whatever it was, he had experienced it before, precisely as it was unfolding before him now. Only now he wasn't comatose. He wasn't even sleeping.

He could remember Katie and the girls sitting on the sofa, just as they were at this moment. The doorbell rang and then the screams ... he woke to the screams. Good screams. Good screams that hadn't started out that way.

Zach peered out the bay window of the living room. Gray faded to black, like it had the first time. And then ... "ring, ring."

"I'll get it!" Dove yelled as she popped off the sofa.

"No, I'll get it!" Aria followed.

As the girls dashed across the carpet toward the front door, Katie pressed the pause button on the remote.

"Noooooo!" Zach bellowed out desperately, "Don't answer that door!" He knew they couldn't hear him. He had already escaped this nightmare once before. But this time would be different. He knew, somehow, this time he would finish the dream he had started months ago. Or maybe, it would finish him.

He began to tremble in helpless anticipation. Each breath soured with fear, each heartbeat rattled his ribcage. He was about to discover who, or what, was at the door and he knew that whomever … or whatever … it was had come for him.

Aria turned the knob and pulled the door slowly open. "Can I help you?"

"Yes, can we help you?" Dove echoed from behind.

Zach peered over his daughters' heads as fear oozed from unfinished memory. It was Judith … Judith Sample. She stood expressionless in the doorway as the rain that drenched her hair trickled over her forehead. She was dressed in the same black gown she had worn to the Reese party … the night she died. Only now, the gown was torn and tattered and soiled with stale blood. All of its splendor … all of her splendor … ravaged by what he had done to her.

Judith stared in at Zach who stood behind the sofa. Only she was aware of his presence. And only she could hear the words he mumbled as his voice withdrew against his fear, "But it wasn't my fault!"

Suddenly the screams of his family, the ones that had rescued him from this scene once before, were detonated by the terror that never evolved the first time he was here. This time, however, Zach wasn't waking up.

Something was happening to this stranger at the door, something hideous. Katie tried to force the door closed but some unseen power held it in place. She corralled the girls by their shoulders and jerked them back away from it with such intensity; the three of them tumbled to the floor. The stranger stepped inside and the door slammed shut behind her.

Judith's eyes changed first, from sparkling green to infinite black, stealing the mood from the weather outside. They stared through him unmercifully. A dark fury raged within.

Then, something began to protrude out from her neck, just below her left ear. The slender form burrowed along beneath her skin and revealed the shape of a small snake. The head navigated its way up one cheekbone and across her forehead as her skin expanded, then contracted, like elastic around it. As the form undulated down her other cheek, Judith opened her mouth, exposing the decayed wolf-like canines that lined her gums and the strands of saliva that now dangled past her chest.

Katie and the girls huddled unnoticed on the floor against the entertainment center. Zach could only watch the unholy transformation from the confines of starched panic that restrained him behind the sofa. Judith's focus was etched into his stiff frame like some ancient alphabet into a tablet of stone.

The serpent that had moved about beneath her skin emerged from her gaping mouth and slithered down over her chin. As it started down her neck beneath the high collar of her gown, Judith snapped her jaws closed, severing the scaled creature in two and sending a searing jolt of pain through Zach's groin. He shrieked and his knees buckled.

He caught himself going down, employing the back of the sofa to hoist himself into a loosely erect position. His left arm hooked to the sturdy piece of furniture and he struggled to stay upright against the gravity of pain that pulled him toward the floor. He winced in agony as he brought his right hand up from the crotch of his tattered jeans. *Blood.* There was blood on his fingers, blood that seeped through the threads of his pants, blood that unveiled the remarkable power of the evil that stood before him.

Judith began to giggle fiendishly. She too was marked with blood, blood that was smeared across her mouth and chin. She used her tongue to clear some of it away from her cracked lips. Was it the snake's blood, or his?

Then, as if her lungs were filling with helium, she rose up off the floor. She stood on nothing but air, suspended like an angry ghost several inches above the plush living room carpet. Carried on the saddle of a delicate breeze that ruffled her gown slightly, she started to drift forward.

Katie and the girls continued to scream. Zach pulled himself upright and attempted to flee. Pain stabbed at his groin with every cowardly twitch as Judith stopped a mere five feet away from him.

Suddenly, with the velocity of a rejected stone being slung from the belly of a tornado, she shot across the remaining distance between them. Zach hadn't time to even turn away as the approaching blur slammed into him.

Absorbing every inch of her unconstrained fury, he tumbled backwards onto the floor behind the sofa, blacking out on impact. But not completely. All feeling went numb. All sight was eclipsed. All sound fell silent. All sound ... except for the faint screams of Katie and the girls.

Chapter Twenty-Seven

Thoughts trickled back into Zach's brain, unannounced, like a sudden spell of hiccups. He was lying on his back and the scent of formaldehyde bleached the air he inhaled into his aching lungs. Beyond that, little else was obvious. Only that he felt as if he had been asleep for months, maybe years.

He peeled his flinching lids from eyes that hadn't breathed for what seemed like an eternity; and the slightest tinge of light forced them shut instantly. He coerced them open once more, gaining the day's final reflection from the sun that was dropping behind the hills outside his window. His blurred vision rubbed like sandpaper against the light being cast from the fluorescent fixture above him as it gradually translated abstract configurations into discernible details.

It was a hospital room. He was in the hospital. But why? His brain labored to recall. Flashes of recollected images offered their explanation in pieces.

Judith. He was attacked by Judith, or whatever it was that she had become right there in front of him, in front of his family. He could summon only the final seconds of the incident from his clouded memory. The living room, her slamming into him, the screaming, that was it. He blacked out and only the screams filtered through.

How much time had passed? He could only guess. A year? Two years? But the screams, it seemed, lasted mere seconds. And now he was awake. Or was he? All concept of time was muffled. All else was too.

As his senses sharpened with the fading of unconsciousness, familiar voices emerged from the idle of confusion. "He's waking up nurse, go get the Doctor."

Zach turned his head toward the voice and Katie appeared. She was sitting on the edge of the bed, tears leaking from around her eyes.

"Hi baby," she quivered as she waved her hand in front of Zach's pale face, "Oh, thank God … Can you hear me, Zach?"

Dove and Aria were there too, smiling. Zach nodded, managing something of smile in return. He attempted to speak. The stale words stuck in his throat.

"Shhhhh!" Katie instructed. "Just rest, the doctor is on his way."

Rest! It felt like he'd been resting for the better part of a political term. Besides, questions had to be answered.

"You're okay?" he whispered, finally able to summon soft speech. "The girls?"

"We're fine, now stop straining yourself," Katie said, wiping her eyes with her thumb.

"But you did see her, right?" he continued against Katie's wishes. "You saw her?"

Katie knew the best thing was for Zach not to speak, but her curiosity pushed the question to the point of asking, "Who?"

"The woman that …" his words tapered off as he realized she hadn't seen Judith at all. Realized that he, in fact, was the only one fucked up enough to see monstrous reincarnations of dead people in the living room. If Katie had seen her, she surely wouldn't have to ask who."

"Woman?" she pressed.

Now Zach was really perplexed. If Katie and the girls never saw her, if she indeed was just a character in the macabre melodrama of his madness, how did she put him in the hospital?

"At the house, the one who attacked me! You didn't see her?" He pushed the sketchy details at Katie, hoping to solicit the response he desperately sought but knew wouldn't be offered. Zach could tell by the confusion that crinkled her expression that she had absolutely no idea what he was rambling about. "Then, why am I in the hospital?"

"You were in a terrible accident, back in September," she explained. "You were in a coma up until just a minute ago."

Zach's thoughts withdrew in confused silence. She couldn't be talking about the car accident, could she? "You mean when I rolled the Lexus over the hillside?" his words rose on escalating confusion.

A replay of that horrible night rushed his memory. A dark, rainy evening on an unfamiliar road. The way bolts of lightning split the night sky like an electric saber. Judith slouched in the passenger's seat in a heap of intoxication. And that face. The one he saw right before he woke up at the wheel. *The face of Satan.*

"Yes, Zach," Katie's voice pulled him back into the conversation, "when you rolled the Lexus. You remember it?"

"But I ... I woke from the coma the next day," he insisted. "You were there, the girls, remember?"

"No sweetie, you just woke up a few minutes ago."

"That's not possible," Zach snapped under the strain of a weak voice. He had to defend what little sanity he could still lay claim to. His brain scrambled for something to convince Katie. "What about Aria's birthday?" he submitted after several moments of jumbled deliberation. I was there. We had that stupid dinosaur at the house ..."

"Dinosaur?" Katie probed gently, not wanting to upset this man in his delicate condition, this man who was obviously confused. "No baby, we had Aria's birthday at my sister's this year."

"Yeah, Daddy, I was real sad you missed it," Aria chimed in, bearing further witness to her mother's testimony as she twirled a stray thread from her little peach dress in one tiny finger. "You'll just have to buy me an extra present next year."

"Your sister's? But I ..." Zach's argument seeped into the giant vacuum of uncertainty that was sucking up every last dust bunny of reason. He raised his head up off his pillow, but only for a moment, as the cobwebs in his brain, which felt like they had been spun out of lead, pulled it quickly back down.

"Relax sweetie," Katie advised. "We'll talk about it later."

Relax! Stubborn women. He just wasn't getting through to them. He had to have been awake. It was all too real. But then again … demons, monsters, real. Now that didn't add up to a nickel's worth of sense, did it? Everything he had been through, none of it made any sense. And this explained it all. Katie was right. She had to be. He had been in a coma.

The last five month gob of his life had been nothing more than a very real, very convincing dream; a dream whose depths could only be reached in the darkest recesses of a coma. Now, he just had to convince himself of that.

Chapter Twenty-Eight

Four days later

Zach shifted his shoulders against the stack of pillows that propped him into an awkward sitting position in his bed. The television on the wall scattered silent, unconsumed images across the room as a turquoise clad nurse's aid collected unconsumed scraps of hospital fare on the tray in front of him.

"I'll just get this out of your way," she informed, balancing the tray on one arm as she adjusted the glasses that kept sliding down her slender nose. "The nurse will be down in a bit."

"Thank you," Katie said from the chair on the opposite side of the bed nearest the window. "They say you'll be able to come home in about a week," she turned her attention to Zach as the nurse's aid scurried through the door into the hallway.

"I sure as hell can't wait to get out of this place." He shifted once more for support. "This damn bed is giving me a stiff spine."

The injuries Zach had sustained in the car accident healed completely while he slept away the last five months and neither the accident nor the resulting coma damaged his brain permanently. Just headaches and the occasional spells of dizziness and confusion that passed when he closed his eyes for a few seconds. Dr. Kim labeled the total recovery "a product of divine medicine."

Zach was still spaghetti on his feet and it would take several weeks for the starch to return to his stride but, when it did, he would be sturdy as a Clydesdale again.

"Would you like another pillow?" Katie asked, reading the bold print headline of discomfort on Zach's face. "I think there's another one in the cabinet."

"No, no, it won't do any good. These damn things are like burlap sacks filled with charcoal."

"Like airplane pillows," Katie snickered, unable to pry even the slightest twitch from the dry corners of Zach's mouth.

His mood was crankier than an antique victrola and the music it played was not meant for dancing. With each passing day, each passing hour, his desire to be released from the hospital swelled. As far as he was concerned, there was absolutely no reason why he had to stay, even though Dr. Kim had explained that they needed to keep an eye on him for a little while longer. And why did he still need this irritating IV jammed into the tender bruise on the back of his left hand?

It was not, however, merely the lack of home-appointed amenities that had been troubling him for the last four days and continued to nag him much more than any needle. "I know I've seen this room before," he remarked as he struggled into yet another uncomfortable position. "I've been here before!"

"A hospital room's a hospital room babe; you've probably been in a dozen just like it."

"Uh, uh, it was this room!" he snapped as he pulled his right hand, the one not hooked up to the IV tube, out from under the sheets and pointed deliberately around the room. "That television! That window! This bed!"

Katie snarled under her breath as she reached across the bed for the unopened carton of milk the nurse's aid had left on the rolling table that stretched out under Zach's chin. She used her thumbs to open it, and then took a sip. "Remember what Dr. Kim said. When a person is as deep as you were, they sometimes dream very convincing dreams, even see little glimpses of the future."

"Little glimpses?" Zach repeated sarcastically. "And what about the rest of it? Christ, I experienced five months of little glimpses, lived and breathed five months of little glimpses!"

Katie was becoming annoyed with Zach's moodiness and her own wearisome anxiety stuck like an August heat that would whittle away at anyone's tolerance threshold.

Still, she did not lash back at him. She knew that he was going through a tough time; and besides, she was too damn tired for an argument. Instead, she took another sip of the milk, which tasted more like non-dairy creamer, then lifted herself slowly out of the chair. She placed the open milk carton back on the rolling table before bending over to peck Zach on the forehead. "I don't know baby, but it's getting late and I have to pick the girls up from my sister's before they get too snugly on her big llama skin rug."

Zach reached out and grabbed her hand, "I'm sorry I'm being such a grump. My head is just so damn screwed up right now and I'm sick of this place already and ..."

"You don't need to explain," Katie interrupted. "You've been to hell and back, I understand." She pulled her purse from the wide window ledge, hooked the strap onto her shoulder, and tucked the bag between her elbow and ribs. She walked lazily around to the other side of the bed. "I'll be back in the afternoon tomorrow, probably around one. You get some rest."

"Tell the girls Daddy loves them," he requested as Katie made her way toward the hallway. She did not bring Dove and Aria to visit Zach this evening because they had been there the previous three days and she felt four days in a row in a dreary hospital room was a bit much for two little girls who were bored and fidgety before hugs and kisses wore off.

"I will," she waved and then disappeared around the corner. But something more than the faint scent of her perfume stayed with him after she left the room. It was something she said. *Hell and back.* He had indeed been to hell. She couldn't have been more right about that. Met the Prince of Darkness himself as a matter of fact, even if it all was just a dream. But the part about him being back ... she could not have been more wrong about that.

Chapter Twenty-Nine

Zach felt blindly for the button that would turn off the television and complete the darkness around him. As his fingertips read like jumbled Braille the remote built into the bed guard, however, something kept him from pressing what may or may not have been the appropriate bump. "You were not in Hell," the television spoke … to him. It was a familiar voice, one he hoped, even started to believe, he would never hear again.

"Wha..wha..what?" his own voice trembled as he glanced up at the screen and saw the old priest, Kazcmarek, staring down at him from the nineteen-inch square of glass.

"I said you were never in Hell. You haven't gotten quite that far yet."

Zach's fingers, which remained on the surface of the remote control pad, began to push frantically at every protrusion they rubbed across. One summoned the nurse on duty with the indicator that flickered red above his cracked-open door. Another churned the motor of his adjustable mattress and nearly folded him in half before several more pokes flattened him out again. None of the buttons he pressed, however, would turn off the terrifying image of the old priest or mute the doom he was there to deliver.

"Relentless and without hope or mercy, that is Hell. A much more intense, complete suffering than any you've known before, one that drowns you in your own sweat and tears and urine and never lets you come up for air," Kazcmarek's voice seemed to crackle with pleasure as he continued. "What you have experienced to this point has merely been ... well let's just call it your place in line, your seat in the lobby."

Zach said nothing. He was not able to speak and he had abandoned all attempts to turn the television off or change the disturbing channel. He only laid there, his hands clinched into fists so tight, his fingerprints were sure to be stamped into his palms. There was nothing he could do, only listen. The message would be delivered in its entirety; and whether he wanted to receive it or not, he would hear every ominous word. "But now your time has come, your wait is over. Our wait is over."

With that, the television flicked off and Kazcmarek was gone. It was in the few moments of darkness that followed that Zach could sense the end. He was so close to Hell itself, he could feel the immense heat of its raging fires scorching his soul. Broken syllables fractured the sentences he could not say, the questions he could not ask. Besides, there was nobody there to answer them, nobody until ...

The door of his room swung open with a squeal and the light popped on above him. "You called, Mr. Bell?" The false comfort of the nurse's voice gained his attention as he turned his head to discover it wasn't the nurse who spoke to him at all ... *it was Katie*.

Why was his wife's presence not a relief? Why was it, in fact, even more frightening than when Kazcmarek, the courier of such terror, such doom, suddenly appeared in the room without even having to use the door?

Something inside told him that this was not really his loving wife of nearly a decade, the mother of his two beautiful daughters. Maybe it was the smirk on her face, a sinister curling at the corners of her mouth and the squinting of eyes that seemed to burn right through his soul like laser beams. Maybe it was that she had left only fifteen minutes earlier and was now back, wearing a nurse's outfit. She never was the kinky type. And what was she holding behind her back? Something small and shiny. A needle?

Katie strolled up to Zach's bedside, a model on the runway of some sinister fashion gala. She stood there, smiling and gazing down upon him as he turtled in fear at the far edge of the bed, nearly tumbling to the floor on the other side. "What's the matter Zach, not happy to see me?"

"What are you doing here? Visiting hours are over."

Katie's tone suggested great amusement, "Oh, I just forgot something is all."

"Why are you wearing that outfit and … and … what are hiding behind your back?"

"What, you don't like this outfit? You don't think I look sexy? Not like Judith, huh? Or one of your other whores!" For a moment she stood above him in silence, gauging his reaction and indulging in the horrified surprise it revealed. Her eyes widened to take in more of his desperation, "Yes baby, I know all about her. I always knew. And that other secretary slut, Alicia. Oh, and the blonde bimbos, Shelli and Stephanie and … and who was the one from Toledo? The one you called ShuggyBear? You remember, the one who liked it up the ass?"

"What are you talking about Kate?" he tried to mask the shock that smattered his face with guilt, but it was useless.

"Nikki!" she blurted out as she pulled her right hand around, exposing the needle she had partially hidden behind her back, "It was Nikki, wasn't it?"

"What are you gonna do with that?" His trembling became obvious and uncontrolled.

"IT WAS NIKKI, WASN'T IT?" She pushed on the syringe, expelling a stream of liquid from the tip of the needle.

"Okay, alright, it was Nikki. I'm sorry. Please just put that thing down."

But Katie wasn't going to put it down. She wasn't going to listen to this unfaithful wretch who had been deceiving her all of these years, who had started fooling around on her practically before the honeymoon souvenirs had even started to collect dust on their mantel. She wasn't going to have pity on him and she wasn't going to hear anymore of his bullshit. And he knew it.

As Katie raised her arms toward the ceiling, holding the needle in a two fisted grip over her head like a Samurai sword, Zach squeezed his eyes shut. He knew she was there for only one reason. She was going to jam that needle into his chest. She was going to inject that poison right into his most vital organ. Right into his heart. She was, in fact, going to kill him.

* * *

Zach opened his eyes as reality settled urgently back into place. Unmistakable, unadulterated reality. The pounding of heavy raindrops that splattered off the windshield and the polished voices that echoed from the speakers. The shrieking wail of tires and the dizzying whirl of lost control. It all came charging back into his brain in a jumbled heap. The spinning chaos. The panic.

For Zachary Bell, life had never been more real than at this very moment. And neither had death. A dark silhouette closing in like certain road kill. The green glow of that final terrified glance. The eyes of doom caught in the swirl of headlights.

Wherever he had been, he was back now, in the last fleeting seconds of his earthly existence. His body had never left the driver's seat of his Lexus after Reese's party. But his soul most certainly had. He had indeed fallen asleep at the wheel and his body was about to become a torn and mangled heap among the metal carnage of a crumpled sedan.

For his soul, however, the previous few seconds had been a five month journey, with Satan at the wheel. It had all been merely a dream; and yet, it was everything he had seen, everything he had experienced, everything he had never truly understood. It had been a preview of his afterlife, his eternal damnation.

The Lexus slid in chaotic pirouettes across rain-soaked blacktop as the tires answered the desperation of trampled breaks with a helpless squeal. The world around it was a kaleidoscope of swirling scenery, an uninterrupted sequence of briefly illuminated images.

Zach too was helpless. The car had already begun to hydroplane before he even realized that he and Judith Sample were still in a car, and his grip was insubstantial against the forceful pull of the steering wheel. As the Lexus spun toward the unguarded hillside, he knew they were going to go over the edge. He had, after all, been through this accident before. But then again, not really. Not until now.

Zach locked himself into a rigid posture and squeezed his eyes shut. An image flashed in his mind from out of the darkness. The pentagram with a Roman numeral at each point. IX, I, III. September 13. He had seen the symbol three times before: on the wall at the hospital, on the wall behind Katie during Thanksgiving dinner, and on the windshield of his car the night he tried to kill himself—although each of those events had taken place only in his mind. But this was the first time he was able to decipher its ominous meaning, a meaning that became obvious in a single chaotic instant. The numerals represented today's date, September 13 ... *the date of his death.*

The Lexus slid over the embankment and began its tumbling decent toward Gus Hadley's front lawn like a steel gymnast. Judith Sample's limp, unbelted body was tossed to the back seat. Her neck snapped, absorbing the weight of her entire mass as her head slammed against the rear window. She never felt a thing. The rum induced slumber assured her that comfort.

Zach, however, could hear the initial submission of metal as it buckled around him, squeezing shattered glass from its yielding frame. But the silence came swiftly, as it had before, with a solid thump. His skull slammed off the bowed roof with such force, it nearly collapsed around his brain.

After two cartwheels, two somersaults, and a single airborne twist, gravity finally collected the mangled heap on Gus Hadley's front lawn. The creak of relaxing metal was joined by a subtle hiss as the radiator exhaled gray smoke from under the hood.

A trio of farm dogs howled with anxious curiosity into the disturbed night. Even the hillside was alive as unscathed trees rustled amongst themselves in animated relief. But from inside the cab of the twisted Lexus, there was nothing. No sound. No movement. No life.

Lights popped on inside the crooked little wooden house acrosss the way, mapping the slow path of its occupant through the screened windows, from the second floor to the first and then, after several moments, onto the porch. The old farmer stood for a minute on the splintering planks that groaned beneath his weight, swatting at insects and peering out into the hazy darkness, then staggered across his lawn with lingering sleep in his eyes and a bottle of Scotch in his hand.

He stopped a few paces from the wreckage and gazed at the contorted heap of metal that appeared to have been tossed out of Heaven and into his front yard. Squinting through cataracts and rain-splattered glasses, the old man could make out the two lifeless bodies inside. He could see no movement at all.

Movement, however, was not the only thing he was unable to see. There was something else. Something he could never have seen, never have witnessed, not even on the clearest of nights, not even through the youngest of eyes.

Zach sat dazed against the trunk of a large oak tree only a few feet away. He had crawled from the wreckage, passing directly through the driver's side door like a phantom without substance. No bone. No muscle. No skin. He had left all that weight behind in the driver's seat of the car. His body had been abandoned, torn and bloody, pinned in an upright pose that suggested he would simply drive away from the scene at any moment. That was, if the steering wheel hadn't been pressed into his chest.

Zach's battered, lifeless body would not be going anywhere until Fire Rescue arrived to extract it from the jagged metal more than an hour later. Zach's soul, however, wouldn't have to wait that long.

When Zach's disengaged spirit called out from beneath the tree to the old man who was now turning back toward his house to call the State Police, Gus Hadley heard only the gentle beat of rain drops all around him and the distant cacophony of agitated hounds beyond the darkness. And when Zach let out the first desperate screams as something snaked up out of the earth, wrapped around his wrists and ankles like scaled fingers that had clawed up through the stratosphere, and began to pull his condemned soul down into a scorching inferno, old Gus was never aware that another seat, possibly his own, had just been vacated in the lobby of Hell.

Afterlife
Evil men do not understand justice, but those who
seek the Lord understand it fully.
   —Proverbs 28:5

For the wage of sin is death, but the gift of God
is eternal life in Jesus Christ our Lord.
   —Romans 6:23

With flesh, one is given mortality. With blood, the promise of death. This is Adam's law. A sentence imposed in the first breath, effected in the last. But with each that is spent in between, man must stand trial for his soul. For while the revocation of the body is the penalty for humanity, the soul is restitution paid by those without faith.

Printed in the United States
127874LV00001B/350/P